Charlie on

*'Being almost fourteen's not all it's c____
a girl.'*

Charlie has a lot of problems thes__
and has given up her job on the __
new-man Jed, is going to ante-na_____ ____ ___ __as started to
__ffer from morning sickness. And of course Mum has decided
_____ ll going to move to the country.

____while, Mum has taken over the school pantomime which
____inks is sexist, cast Charlie as the policeperson, and showed
___ White how to defend herself from sexual harassment from
___ince.

22. ___ in the middle of all this, how is Charlie going to get the pair
___otted shoes she longs for? How is she going to become an
___r? And above all, how is she going to get her first kiss from
___ alleged boy-friend, Gazza?

__ Welford was born in Sussex and trained to be a secretary
___re giving up work to bring up her children. When they
___ed school, she had several part-time jobs, and then became an
___torial writer with a local newspaper. When she was made
___undant, she continued writing at home and had several
___cles published in magazines. After five rejected novels, her
___ book for young adults was published in 1989. *Charlie on the
__ol* is the fifth of her books to be published by Oxford University
__ss.

__ue has lots of interests: writing, writing and . . . writing. She
__o enjoys rummaging around antique shops, researching local
__story, and walking her two Jack Russell terriers.

___arlie in the Pink
__N 0 19 271698 0

__unny home-and-school story with a trendy theme: Mum is a
__n feminist; step-dad is a New Man.'

The Economist

__éminist mother rearing a traditionally conventional daughter
__.good joke skilfully and believably developed.'

Junior Bookshelf

__t in the Mirror
__ 19 271704 9

__cy mixture of mystery, everyday grittiness, and romance.'

Sunday Times

Charlie on the Spot

Other books by Sue Welford

Ghost in the Mirror
Snowbird Winter
The Night after Tomorrow
Charlie in the Pink

Charlie on the Spot

Sue Welford

Oxford University Press

Oxford New York Toronto

Oxford University Press, Walton Street, Oxford OX2 6DP

Oxford New York Toronto
Delhi Bombay Calcutta Madras Karachi
Kuala Lumpur Singapore Hong Kong Tokyo
Nairobi Dar es Salaam Cape Town
Melbourne Auckland Madrid

and associated companies in
Berlin Ibadan

Oxford is a trade mark of Oxford University Press

A CIP catalogue record for this book is available
from the British Library

Cover design Slatter-Anderson
Printed and bound in Great Britain by
Biddles Ltd, Guildford and King's Lynn

1

Being almost fourteen's not all it's cracked up to be. Especially if you're a girl.

Here are a few of the reasons:

1) Your boobs don't grow very fast.
2) Your hormones give you acne and period pains.
3) Gorgeous Gazza's really more interested in football than he is in you.
4) Your mum decides to move to the country.
5) Second-hand green wellies don't go with your perfectly wonderful pink frock.
6) You're supposed to decide (in my case my *mum's* supposed to decide) what career you want when you leave school. (Being a wife and mother apparently doesn't count.)
7) You start to sweat and have to take a deodorant to school. (Everyone laughed because I'd pinched my mum's and they said Jumbo-stick for that jungle freshness smelt like elephant's pooh. When I said she used it because it wasn't tested on animals, they said it was probably *for* animals.)

8) You start to grow hair in funny places.

I looked in my *True Life Affair* magazine for answers.

I remember my form teacher Miss Lamb (Mary Hadda to us) telling me that there was nothing you couldn't find out if you had the right book. That was the day I spotted a copy of *The Joy of Sex* in her vanity case.

All my *magazine* told me was how to lose weight, how to put sizzle into your sex life (which, as I haven't got a sex life, wasn't really relevant), and how to keep your skin looking lovely on the Costa del Sol. As I'm totally skinny, the losing weight bit was totally boring. And I've never been to the Costa del anything so that was a waste of 65p. Mind you, as my real dad had given me the money to buy a new lipstick, it didn't really matter.

My real dad likes girls to look like girls.

I tried to tell him about this bloke on TV who wears lipstick all the time, and mascara, but he didn't listen. I think the sound of Murray Walker commentating on the Grand Prix and the yelling of his wife Blossom's gorgeous, fragrantly sweet new baby, Petal, drowned my words.

As usual, my mum announced it over breakfast.

'OK, Charlie . . . Jed . . .' (Jed's my mum's toy-boyfriend, just a step away from being my step-dad. He's a New Man. Not new to my mum because they've been living together for two years.) ' . . . pack up our stuff, we're moving.'

Oh no, I thought, not again.

I yawned. Bored with the conversation already.

Back in the summer, Al had got a bee in her helmet about becoming New Age Travellers. We were on the brink of setting off for Stonehenge when she changed her mind. I think it might have had something to do with Jed's refusal to have half his head shaved, even though his perm had grown out. And I knew he hated DMs and

2

jeans that had holes in. He said they were too clumsy for someone of his slender build. (The boots, not the jeans.) He also knew that the compulsory scruffy mongrel dog would bring him out in blotches.

Anyway, Mum sent the converted ambulance back to the hospital and hoped they wouldn't notice she'd swapped the stretchers and oxygen unit for bunks and a cooker. Later she remembered she'd left her Elvis look-alike mask in one of the overhead first-aid compart-ments. She'd had it repaired since the branch fell on it whilst we were camping in Toadstool Wood. I *thought* I'd seen a dark-haired ambulance man with a guitar and sideburns driving around town.

'Moving?' Jed put down his Chippendales mug full of ginger, banana-peel and knapweed herbal tea. He looked confused. 'When, where . . . ?'

'To the country.' Mum slammed her Glucoseade for super-energy can down on the table and took a last mouthful of Sainsbury's luxury muesli. 'I'd bawt tiss cotm in Pwath Btm.'

'What?' I looked up from my *Sexy Lover* mag. Luckily Mum hadn't spotted I was reading it. It must have been my lucky day. I'd warned the paper-girl to wrap it in an old *Wrestling and Body Beautiful* magazine cover but she'd forgotten.

Al swallowed noisily. When she'd finished coughing up bits of peanuts and wheatgerm, she said, 'I've bought this cottage in Pratts Bottom with the dosh I got from my TV appearance.'

'Which one?' Jed asked.

He took the headphones out of his ears and switched off his Des O'Connor tape. As usual, he caught one of the wires in his ear-ring. Wincing, he managed to get it out before any real damage was done. It could have been blood on his ear-lobe but it was more likely a blob of coloured hair-gel for Men Who Need That Extra Hint-of-a-Tint. It hadn't been tested on animals, of course.

3

It hadn't been tested on anyone by the look of Jed's hair.

'That Channel 4 programme about sexual equality and serial killers, surely you remember, sweetie?' My mum stroked Jed's hair and fiddled playfully with his pony tail.

'No, dearest . . .' Jed replied patiently, 'which *cottage*?'

'Oh . . .?' My mum took a grubby, torn piece of paper from the top pocket of her boiler suit. 'This one,' she frowned. ' I do wish these estate agents would use recycled paper to print their fantasies on.'

Jed gazed at the piece of paper then handed it to me. On it was a picture of something closely resembling a wooden shack. He still looked confused.

Blinking long-lashed eyes up at her he said, 'But . . . ' Then seeing a frown darken her dark eyebrows he went on, 'But . . . it's lovely, sweetie, look at that fabulous, exotic garden, Charlie. '

All I could see was a jungle. 'We're not going to live in *that*, are we?' I asked innocently.

'Yes. And what's wrong with it, my girl? Some people don't have any—'

I knew what she was going to say.

'Yes, Mum . . . ' I interrupted. People don't usually interrupt my mum but she *was* late for her job on the building site so I knew I was in with a chance. 'But it does need doing up . . . look . . . '

'For Sympathetic Renovation' was printed underneath the picture.

'Well, I can do all the DIY while Jed keeps house. No arguments now, Charlie . . . I've decided it's better to bring children up in the country . . . more healthy. All that fresh air and dung heaps. I haven't campaigned endlessly for the preservation of our rural heritage just for everyone else to get the benefit.' She took her helmet and leather jacket from under the sink. With difficulty, she shrugged her jacket on over the shoulder pads in her

4

boiler suit. She'd put on a lot of weight since she swapped aerobics for Sumo wrestling classes. 'We're not green for nothing, are we, Charlie?'

'No, Mum.' I took off my baseball cap. My head felt all itchy. Maybe the hat belonged to someone with fleas before I got it? Actually, I was sure I'd got dandruff, although the extract of beetroot shampoo I'd got from the 'Glamour without Pain' shop said it would cure it. Even if it didn't, it made your hair a lovely colour — a kind of mixture between blood and deadly-nightshade berries.

'I'm signing the contracts today.' My mum picked up a brown envelope from beside her copy of *Liberated Woman* magazine. It had some kind of official stamp on the front (the envelope not the magazine). 'And they can whistle for this.' She threw the final rent demand into the garbage bin. 'Damn property barons . . . ' she muttered. 'Coming, Jed?'

Jed clutched his mobile phone to his chest. 'But I haven't done the washing up,' he wailed.

'Never mind,' Mum said. 'It'll still be here when you get home from the office.' She bent to kiss me. 'Now don't you do it, Charlie, I know what you're like. Jed will have plenty of time before he gets dinner.' She took a step backwards, frowning again. At first I thought she'd seen my magazine but she said, 'Charlie, what's that sticking out of the top of your Turtle?'

(I've got this green Hero Turtle back-pack for my school stuff.) 'Er . . . it's my cookery things, Al,' I stammered. Al is my mum's name. She really prefers me to call her that. She says women who are merely thought of as mothers have no real identity.

Al kicked the tin with the steel toecap of her boot. 'You haven't got cookery again, Charlie?' She sighed. 'I don't know, won't they ever teach girls anything useful.'

'The boys do it as well, ' I piped up.

'Yes, but how many *girls* are in the school tug-of-war team?'

'Er . . . none.'

There weren't any boys either but if I told her she'd only start one up. Our school had never been the same since she insisted on unisex changing rooms. For one thing, Sharon Smith *never* came out.

Al scratched her head, just above her ear where she'd had all her hair shaved off apart from the words 'Elvis for Ever' dyed purple. Round the other side she wanted the barber to put 'Stop the Bloody Fur Trade' but there wasn't room. He only had room to put 'Stop the Blood . . .' If you read it all round it says 'Stop the Blood Elvis for Ever'.

'Anyway, Mum,' I went on, 'I like cookery.'

'I know that, Charlie, but surely Astronomical Navigation would be more useful to someone who's going to be an airline pilot or a structural engineer?'

'Astronomical Navigation's not in the National Curriculum, Mum.'

She snorted. 'We'll have to see about that then, won't we?'

I sighed again. 'Not another campaign, please, Mum.'

'Why not, Charlie, losing your bottle?'

I looked in my Turtle but there was only a can of Coke.

'Mum, we *are* making Black Forest Gateau,' I said, knowing chocolate was just one of my mum's weaknesses. Along with martial arts, arm wrestling, and Hotstuff aftershave . . . and New-Man Jed, of course.

'Well, I hope you're using polyunsaturated fat and organic flour,' she said. She tried to zip up her jacket. 'By the way, don't forget it's my tap-dancing class tonight.'

Jed finished looking in the mirror and put away his oven gloves. He went up to the bedroom. We could hear the sweet sound of Des O'Connor floating down the stairs. Jed came down wearing his designer lilac suede jacket. It really didn't go with those yukkie green trousers but I didn't say anything. I mean, who was I to criticize? My grey leggings, white fluffy tank top, age 10

6

school blazer, and red baseball cap were hardly the height of fashion. Nor were my second-hand Reeboks I'd had for years. At least they fitted me now. They'd been three sizes too big when Al brought them home. Someone had chucked them in a skip outside the building site where she works. I reckoned it really was about time I got a new pair — or, more likely, a second-hand pair.

'I'm all yours, sweetie,' Jed said. He took a duster from the cupboard and hurriedly polished the studs on Al's jacket.

'Mum . . . ? Do we really have to move? I like it here.'

I'd suddenly realized the enormity of her statement. I was thinking of me and Jed having to pack up all our stuff double-handed while she dismantled her Kawasaki in the kitchen for the fourteenth time in recent history or practised her tap routine upstairs. A pretty dodgy exercise when you've put on two stone.

'Yes, Charlie, we do.' She gave me a bear hug. 'You might even consider being a farmer or a tractor driver when we get there. Just as a temporary measure, of course, before you're accepted into Flight School or the Institute of Structural Engineers. And as I said, it's more healthy for children to be brought up in the country.'

'But, Mum, I'm nearly *fourteen*, I've *been* brought up,' I spluttered.

Al looked at me from beneath her bright orange, scrunched-up fringe. It seemed to stay more scrunched than ever under the rim of her World War Two soldier's motor-bike helmet. There was a look in her eyes I'd never seen before. It could have been her new long-lash green mascara or maybe she was just getting short sighted.

'Not *you*, Charlie,' she said, smiling. She patted her fat stomach. 'What do you think this is, Charlie? Scotch mist?'

I shrugged, not knowing what she was on about as usual.

7

Al smiled again. Jed winced as she squeezed his arm. She kissed him on the top of his head and when he recovered his balance, she said, still grinning, 'We're having a baby, Charlie — didn't we tell you?'

2

I think that day must have been almost the best day of my almost-fourteen years. I suppose the very *best* day had really been when I took gorgeous Gazza to the disco and he whispered stuff about my boobs growing inside my flouncy pink party frock. But this was almost as good, My mum, having a *baby*! I couldn't wait to tell Gazza the news.

I met him in our usual place. That's one of the great things about having a boyfriend. You have things like 'usual places' to meet. And you have little favourite sayings like 'Oh, Gazza, you are the most wonderful, hunky boy in the entire universe,' and 'Sorry, Charlie, I'm playing soccer every night this week,' and 'Oh, Charlie, you've spent all your pocket money on me again.'

Gaz was kicking his football along the canal when I scooted up on my bike. I hadn't been able to ride it for months. One puncture's not too bad, but two makes riding impossible. It was pretty hard trying to scoot along with a Hero Turtle back-pack and a cake tin balanced on the crossbar. I'd had to stop off at Tesco's to get some organic flour. They only did it in two-kilo bags so I was having a job to carry it.

'Gazza!'

I swooped up to him. He was so startled his glasses almost fell off. He'd given up on contact lenses after one fell out while he was playing five-a-side tiddlywinks and the opposing team scored a wink with it. Or was it a tiddly? I'm not really sure. The football he was kicking went in a wide arc and landed in the middle of the canal. I got *really* muddy wading in to get it for him.

When I got out, Gazza said, grinning, 'Pooh, Charlie, you're going to stink for the rest of the day. Good job you haven't got your pink frock on.'

As a matter of fact, I had worn it to school once or twice but it looked a bit silly with my green Turtle and second-hand Reeboks.

'I'll have a shower before lessons,' I said, trying to brush the mud and soggy fag-ends off my grey leggings. They'd been white once but Jed put them in the washing machine with my mum's black string vests and suspender belts.

Gazza shrugged indifferently.

The trouble with boyfriends is that they get moody. I first found that out when I met Gazza in the shopping mall one Saturday morning to help him choose a present for his new baby brother. He'd been sulking because his mum wouldn't let him stay up to watch *Dribbling for Beginners* on TV the night before. We ended up with a fuzzy football to hang on the baby's cot and a Manchester United shirt that for some reason fitted Gazza himself instead of the baby. At least that cheered him up.

'Gazza, darling . . . ' I blurted. 'I've got some fantastic news.'

'Oh yeah . . . ' Gazza kicked the ball again. Then he ran off, dribbling along the hedgerow (the ball, I mean).

I picked up his school bag and trotted after him.

'Gazza!'

Gazza turned. The morning light shone on his spotty face. Gazza had only got spots in the last few months.

10

Before that his complexion was as beautiful and angel-clear as that girl on TV who advertises Zit-away zit lotion. Gazza said it was the Zit-away zit lotion that gave him spots in the first place. He pushed his grubby baseball cap to the back of his head and peered at me. I couldn't really describe exactly who he looked like, standing there waiting for me. It was something like that scene from *Nightmare on Elm Street* when Freddy first appears with the light shining behind him and that funny hat on. A kind of heavenly-glow, I suppose. He had baby food down the front of his blazer. (Gazza, not Freddy.)

I reached him and said breathlessly in what I hoped was a sexy voice and thinking that maybe today would be the day he'd give me that first passionate kiss I'd been waiting for, 'My mum's having a baby.' I smiled sweetly. 'Quite soon. She's only just remembered to tell me. Won't it be the most wonderful Christmas present a girl ever had?' I clasped my hands to my hardly-growing boobs.

'Yuk,' Gazza said romantically. 'Babies stink!'

Instead of placing his scrummy lips on mine, setting my skinny legs a-tremble and the blood racing round my body in a fury of passion, like the kids do in *Home and Away*, Gazza picked up the ball and stuffed it into his rucksack. It was as much as I could do to carry it.

'They can't help it,' I breathed, disappointed yet knowing the best was yet to come. (It had actually said that in my *Sexy L.* mag. Horoscope Horace had put 'if you're in a steady relationship the best is yet to come'. My relationship with Gazza was certainly steady— steadily getting nowhere.) '*You'd* stink if you had to wear a nappy all day.'

'Do what?' Gazza said, looking blank.

'Stink.' I beamed coyly. 'Babies . . . you know.'

Gaz curled his lip. He looked really hunky when he did that. A kind of cross between Cliff Richard and Axl Rose.

11

'Yuk!' he said sweetly. He pretended to stick his angel fingers down his throat and made these kind of really sexy vomiting noises. Everything Gazza does is really sexy. I remember one of my mags telling me true love is blind but I didn't really agree with that. I can see Gazza's faults as much as anyone. The thing is . . . he hasn't got any.

'Oh . . . I think it's totally stupendous. It's my wish come true to have a baby to look after.'

Gazza stared at me through his new pink-tinted specs. He said his mum had made him get them. Said they were trendy. Sometimes I think my darling Gazza would believe anything. His innocence just makes him more attractive.

My mum laughed when I told her. 'Nothing like seeing the world through rose-coloured glasses, Charlie,' she remarked acidly. 'Especially if you happen to be unfortunate enough to be a man.'

'Pooh,' Gazza said hunkily.

'Oh, Gaz, I'm sorry I pong so much.'

'If you think you pong, then wait until you get the baby. Then you'll really know what *pong* means!'

By now we were near the school gates. I could see my friend, Amy, trying to squeeze through. And Sharon Smith trying to pull her pink velvet mini-skirt down to cover her green knickers. Gazza was looking at Sharon, his wonderful eyes popping out of his head. He took off his specs and wiped them on his sleeve.

'Don't be so horrible, darling.' I pulled at his blazer so he'd notice who was talking to him. 'Babies are gorgeous and sweet . . . a bit like you.'

I said that because I knew you always had to tell your man exactly what you thought of him.

Gazza strode on ahead, calling out to his mates. His friend Michael Richards (known as Mick-the-Dick) was trying to pinch one of Amy's lunch boxes.

I ran after Gaz, anxious to reassure him. 'Gaz — it will be wonderful, honestly. We can take them out together.'

Pushing a pram with Gazza was another of my dreams. He turned to me, looking blank. 'What?'

'Your baby brother and my mum's baby . . . we can take them for walks.'

'Not likely,' Gazza said. 'You won't catch me pushing no pram.' He ran off.

I sighed. There was no doubt about it, my dreams of a life with Gazza, our cottage, the washing, the ironing, were definitely fading into oblivion.

Wanda Walkman danced past me, her personal stereo strapped to her bum bag.

'Hi, Wanda!' I shouted.

She looked blank. ' Pardon?'

I waited while Amy caught me up. I think it was the ground vibrating with her footsteps rather than a point-three-on-the-Richter-scale type earthquake.

'My mum's having a baby,' I said, helping her stuff her lunch boxes back into her school bags.

'What?'Amy took a last bite of her giant, economy-sized Bounty Bar and licked the coconut from her chins.

'My mum,' I said, 'she's having a baby. I knew she was putting on weight but thought it was those banana and mustard sandwiches she'd taken a fancy to.'

'Blimey,' Amy said. She took the clingfilm off one of her mega cheese sandwiches. 'When?'

'When what?'

'When does she eat banana and mustard sandwiches?'

'All the time,' I said.

'Yummy.' Amy took a mega-bite of her mega-sandwich. 'When'shthebabydue?'

'Around Christmas.'

'Pooh.' Amy put a podgy finger into her mouth to remove a bit of cheese from between her teeth. 'I'd rather have a selection box.'

'You would,' I said sweetly.

'Who'sh the father?' She spat a piece of cheese at me.

I looked at her in horror. 'Who do you think?'

13

Amy shrugged, then tucked her boob-tube back into the waistband of her leopardskin-patterned leggings. 'Dunno,' she said, munching. She picked a morsel of sandwich off the lapel of her blazer and popped it back into her mouth.

'It's Jed, of course. New men can be fathers, you know.'

'My dad says he's a poofter.'

'How can he be?'

'What?'

'A poofter.'

'Who?'

'Your dad.'

'Not my dad, stupid,' Amy said between mouthfuls, 'Jed.'

I shook my head. I really didn't know what Amy was talking about although that wasn't surprising. With two cheese sandwiches stuffed in your mouth — who knows what you're trying to say?

Just then Mary Hadda roared up with her boyfriend. He screeched his sports car to a halt in front of the Main Entrance. When Mary had finished putting on her Stay-all-day crimson lipstick in the rear-view mirror, she kissed him goodbye. When she finished wiping her lipstick off half his face, and straightening her clothes, we heard him roar off. I think the screech of tyres meant he'd missed our PE teacher, Ms Keegan, on her mountain bike. I often thought that if Ms Keegan pedalled along on the road instead of up and down the kerb like that she wouldn't cause such a traffic hazard.

'Hello, Charlie,' Mary said, doing up the top buttons of her blouse.

'Hello, Mar— Miss Lamb. My mum's having a baby.'

Mary made a face. 'Oh dear, is she?'

'Yes, isn't it wonderful?'

'Well . . . yes, if you like that sort of thing, I suppose. I'm not fond of children myself.'

Paddy Powell came up from behind. I think it was disgust on Mary's face as he pinched her bottom. It could have been ecstasy. I'd seen our English teacher John Boy (also known as Mr Walton) pinch her bottom lots of times and she'd looked just the same then.

'Watcha, Charlie,' Paddy sneered. He went a bit cross-eyed trying to focus on the boil on the end of his nose.

'My mum's having a baby at Christmas,' I said.

'Wow!' Paddy shouted. He did a little dance, his hob-nailed DMs beating a rhythm on the playground. I'm sure the tarmac didn't have that great crack in it before. He picked me up by the scruff of my Turtle and swung me round joyously. 'That's great, Charlie! I love babies. Can I come and cuddle it when it's born?' He undid the tab of his can. I don't think Mary Hadda knew she had lager foam all over the back of her hair and I certainly wasn't going to be the one to tell her.

'Of course you can, Paddy darling,' I said, trying to recover my balance. My faith in humanity was restored. I saw Paddy in a new light. Under that torn denim jacket, shaved head, and ear-ringed nose was a heart of gold. I stood on tiptoe to kiss him, then thought better of it. I think it was the yellow tip to his boil that put me off. Anyway, I didn't want Gazza getting jealous, did I? I knew it could be a grave mistake to make your man jealous by kissing someone else, even if it was only because they were pleased you were having a baby.

Paddy grabbed Mick-the-Dick who happened to be trying to push past. 'Watchit, Dick,' Paddy growled. I think Mick was going purple in the face because he couldn't breathe with Paddy hanging on to his tie like that.

'Who's the dad?' Paddy asked, letting Mick go and digging around in his ear for wax. 'That poofter?'

'No,' I said. 'Jed.'

Paddy laughed so much his braces popped off. I can't imagine why. He was just bending down to pick them up

15

when Sammy whizzed through the gates in his wheel-chair. He must have missed Paddy's backside by about half a centimetre.

Sammy gave me a broad grin, then I saw him bounce off Amy and hurtle down the ramp towards Class 3. I bet he was going to finish his homework before school started. I knew he spent all his evenings playing basket-ball at the Sports Centre. Al had towed him home one evening with her bike after her Body Building session.

Just then our new Arts and Drama teacher, Miss Taylor (Known as Sonia Scissorhands. First because her name's Sonia and second on account of her long fingernails.) arrived in her Mini.

'Good morning, Patrick,' she said to Paddy, kicking the car door shut theatrically.

'G . . . good morning, Miss,' Paddy stammered. I know his face was red as a strawberry because he was in love with her. I'd heard him say she could run her fingernails over his tattoos any time. 'Can I carry your portfolio, Miss?'

'Certainly, Paddy.' Sonia Scissorhands gave him an Oscar-winning smile. I saw Paddy jump back in alarm as she waved her hand at him in a gesture of appreciation. If his jacket got any more rips in it, it would fall off completely.

'By the way, Charlie,' Sonia said dramatically. 'I'm casting for the school pantomime at lunchtime. Make sure you come along.'

'Yes, Miss. What're we doing?' I mumbled.

'A pantomime. Are you deaf, Charlie? And I've told you . . . learn to *throw* your voice.' Sonia sliced off the heads of several flowers as she waved her hands in the air.

'No, Miss . . . What pantomime?'

Sonia raised her chin a little higher. '*Snow White and the Seven Dwarfs*, Charlie. The details are in the Art room. I put them there myself.'

I remembered seeing a shredded piece of paper hanging from the notice board.

'My mum won't like that, Miss,' I said.

'Like what, Charlie?' Sonia cleared her throat. She took her antiseptic spray from her bag and squirted some into her mouth. Then she mumbled something about Romeo, Romeo wherefore art thou Romeo, under her breath.

'Like us doing *Snow White*.'

'Why not, Charlie?' Sonia frowned and ran her scissor-hands through her blonde Marilyn Monroe wig.

'She says it's sexist.'

'Nonsense, it's been passed by the censor.'

'No . . . sex*ist*.'

'Oh . . . well, I'm sure if she has any objections she'll tell the PTA.'

'My mum *is* the PTA.'

'Well, tell her to come up and see me sometime. ' Sonia gave me another dazzling Hollywood smile and disappeared up the stairs. I could hear her fingernails scraping the walls all the way to the staffroom.

In maths I made a list.

Things to buy for the baby:

1) A pretty frilly pink frock (I hoped it was a girl).
2) A dear little ironing board to iron Teddy's clothes.
3) Teddy.
4) A sweet bonnet with ribbons.
5) A small Turtle back-pack.

Then I thought my gran would probably send it one anyway so I crossed it off. My gran had got a job lot of Turtles at a jumble sale so she sent one to everyone. Even Jed had one to keep his Apollo Masculine Make-up in.

6) A little chair to go on the back of the Kawasaki.
7) Some dear little fake-fur-lined boots for the winter.

8) Hygienic bottom-wipes for the Fragrant Baby-of-Today.

Then I remembered we were going to live in the country so they would have to be waterproof (the boots not the bottom-wipes). I scribbled a note and sent it back to Amy. Amy had to sit at the back or no one could see the blackboard.

'We're moving to the country,' I put. 'My mum wants the baby to grow up in the fresh air.'

She sent a chocolate-encrusted one back. 'I'll come and visit you. Is there a McDonald's there?'

3

I've decided I want to become an actress. Then I can be Gazza's leading lady:

1) Juliet to his Romeo.
2) Cleopatra to his Antony.
3) Mavis to his Derek.
4) Jerry to his Tom.
5) A Bride to his Dracula.
6) Madonna to his . . . er . . . well, whoever she's going out with at the moment.

And being an actress is an easy career to combine with being a wife and mother. For instance, you can learn your lines while doing the ironing and practise your movements while slaving over a hot cooker or hanging out the washing. And being on the road would be no problem. I could just take Gazza and the children in my Star's trailer and lavish all the love and attention upon them in between takes. Just as if we were at home in our dear little cottage with roses round the door and goal posts on the lawn.

I told Al.

'An *actor*, Charlie,' she said assertively. 'A person who acts. There's no need to make the word female.'

'Sorry,' I said.

'Well, Charlie,' she said thoughtfully, 'what's brought this on?'

I told her about the auditions.

Al shook her head. 'You know there are one or two female actors but if you became an airline pilot you would be pioneering the rise of female equality of opportunity.'

'I know that, Mum,' I said. 'But you know I can't stand heights.'

She shrugged. 'A minor problem. Just don't look out of the window.'

'Couldn't I try acting first?'

She shrugged again. She had just got home from work and was sitting with her boots on the table drinking a litre carton of vitamin-enriched milk while Jed peeled the spuds. She smoothed her black leather maternity smock down over her bump.

'Of course, you realize you'll only be offered tarts or old ladies.'

'What?' I looked up from painting my nails. (I'd found the half-empty bottle of Sunny Apricot one-coat gloss varnish in Mary Hadda's waste bin during break.) Surely we weren't having jam tarts for tea? We hadn't been allowed to eat any sweet stuff since Al announced she was pregnant. 'I don't want to give birth to a child addicted to sugar,' she'd said, emptying her usual packets of low-calorie sweetener into her tea.

'Tarts or old ladies,' she repeated. 'There are no strong parts for women these days. Why do you think I decided to abandon my Hollywood career and go back to humping barrows of cement. Brat pack,' she said, 'eat your hearts out.'

I shrugged. 'You said they wanted you to take your clothes off.'

'Exactly.'

Mum got up and turned on the TV. There was an

20

advertisement for automatic washing powder with some stupid boy tipping it all over the kitchen floor. Al tutted and threw her can of Vitamin C all-natural fizzy fruit drink at the screen.

'That's typical,' she shouted. 'Some male twit thinking you clean the floor with washing powder.' She rose, leaving little piles of brick dust on the tablecloth. 'Give us a shout when dinner's ready, Jed angel-honey. I'm going out to polish the bike.'

Just then the phone rang.

It was Amy.

'Hey,' she said. I could hear cornflakes crackling in the background. 'I got the part.'

'What part?'

'Snow White.'

'Oh, that's great, Amy,' I said. It was probably a tear of anguish I wiped from my cheek. Although it could have been a drop of Mr Muscle telephone cleaner where Jed had been doing the housework. I could just have seen my name in lights over the school gates. CHARLIE SCROGGINS — MEGA-STAR. 'You'll be playing opposite Gazza then,' I managed to say, swallowing my disappointment along with my chewing gum.

'What?' I heard Amy gulp noisily, then the sound of teeth tearing at something or other.

'Gazza — he's playing the prince.'

'Oh, blimey,' Amy chewed. 'Not that prat.'

I didn't answer. I knew you should always defend your man but envy was like a knife in my slightly-expanding breast. I'd auditioned for the part but Sonia Scissorhands said I was too tall. I'd almost said that if she waved her hands around like that near my head then I'd soon be several inches shorter. But there was never any point in being cheeky to schoolteachers. Especially ones with fingernails like razors. Anyway, it's dead unfeminine.

'Never mind, Charlie,' Amy was saying. 'You can be my understudy.' I think she laughed when she said that although she could have been choking on her beefburgers.

'Thanks a bunch,' I said.

'Did you say brunch?' Amy giggled. 'Oh, yes please.'

I went out to the back yard. Al was there sitting in a puddle of oil, polishing her Kawasaki.

'Amy's playing Snow White,' I said tearfully.

'Snow White?'

'Yes, we're doing it for the Christmas panto. Didn't I say?'

'*Snow White and the Seven Small Men!*'

Strange, but I could feel the explosion coming. It kind of rumbled up from Al's stomach and erupted from her mouth like that girl in *The Exorcist* when all that yukky green stuff came out of her mouth. It looked as if she'd had pea-soup for dinner. I didn't think it was very good for pregnant mums to explode but didn't manage to say so in time.

'*Snow White*!!' she thundered blackly. 'A story about a girl who devotes herself to seven small *male* persons! Does their housework and cooking while they go off to some paid employment every day . . . and then swaps them for some stupid prince who sexually harasses her in the woods . . . ? Has the world gone mad, Charlie? Or is it just me?'

I was about to tell her it was probably just her when she opened her mouth for another blast. The tattoo on her forehead stood out like an angry neon sign.

'Who's in charge of this . . . this . . .' For once she seemed at a loss for words.

'Er . . . Sonia Scissorhands,' I stammered.

'A woman?'

'Well, you don't get men called Sonia, now do you, Mum?'

She shook her head in disbelief. I really don't know why. I'd certainly never heard of a bloke called Sonia. If

Al still had her dreadlocks they would have whirled round her head like the sails of a windmill. 'A disgrace to her sex,' she said.

'She said it had been passed by the censor . . .' I began.

'Shut up, Charlie! You've said enough.'

She threw down the old pair of Jed's Paddington Bear boxer shorts she used as a polishing rag and stormed past me. I picked myself up, trying to prise the heel of my tatty black stiletto from the broken chest-expander that had been lying around in the yard for a couple of years. Ever since I'd given up trying and Al had decided 42B was big enough.

Al swept through the back door in a whirlwind of nuts and bolts, metal polish and WD40. I heard her boots clumping along the hallway. Then a clunk as she took off her helmet and chucked it on the floor. I could hear her shouting on the phone. Something about a demo. Oh no, I thought, desperation like lead in my bosom. Not another demo! I could face anything. A lifetime of flatchestedness. Getting my clothes from charity shops. Jed leaving hairs in the sink. Not using environmentally unfriendly aerosol sprays or eating undolphin friendly tuna fish sandwiches, giving the rent money to Greenpeace, Gazza preferring football to my womanly charms. (There was a bit in my *Girly* mag. about men who preferred sport to sex. Something about insecurity and their relationships with their mother. It was all a bit beyond me. Gazza has a very good relationship with his mum. Especially as she gives him money to go to football matches every week to get him out of the way.)

But not another demo.

Anything but that!

I sighed and sat down disconsolately on the broken Super Whizzo Go-Kart Mum had bought me last Christmas. She'd only super-whizzed it up the road once and it fell to bits. I thought she'd have other things to think about now she was with child. A campaign for Natural Childbirth, perhaps? She'd already said she wanted to have the baby at home in the shack we were about to move to. She said she refused to be one of a maternity hospital production-line. Maybe a campaign for *child* equality now that she was to have first-hand experience? Well, second-hand actually. I had been a baby once but she seemed to have forgotten that. (She hadn't fulfilled her potential when I was a baby and had been drowning in a sea of submissiveness and domesticity so maybe that's why she'd forgotten.)

I sighed again. My dreams of being an actor seemed doomed to die before they'd hardly even been born. Amy as Snow White . . . Gazza as the Prince . . . I knew he would look totally stunning in a crown. Just like Prince Charles. I couldn't even get the part of a Small Person if I was too tall to be Snow White. That's if there was to be a pantomime at all once Al had finished with the headmaster. *And* we were moving to the country.

The thought of having to clear the back yard of engine parts, broken body-building equipment, builder's rubble, old washing machines, and patio furniture filled me with horror. I'd be sure to cut my hands and break my fingernails. It was true, my boobs *were* growing but not so anyone would notice. Gazza certainly didn't. The only round things he was interested in were footballs. (Unless you counted Sharon Smith's bottom.) I pulled up my fluffy peach sweater just to make sure my boobs had grown a bit. I could see my reflection in the polished exhaust pipe of Al's Kawasaki. I might be too tall to play a Small Person but I looked like a little twisted pixie in my mum's exhaust pipe. (Not actually *her* exhaust pipe, the one on her motor bike.) I sighed again and fiddled disconsolately with the hole in my black stirrup tights.

Al came storming back, her leather maternity smock flapping about like Dracula's bat-wings.

'Well,' she said smugly. 'That's that.'

'What's what?'

'No need for a campaign this time. I'm taking over the production.' She smiled. 'Of course, with my experience in Hollywood I'm definitely the right man for the job. Meeting of cast and back-stage persons tomorrow — 19.00 hours. Be there, Charlie.'

'But I'm not in it,' I protested.

'Not in it? Don't be silly, Charlie.' She munched on a low-calorie pickled onion and strawberry jam sandwich. 'If you're going to be an actor this could be your big break.'

She went back indoors and I could hear her Guns 'n'Roses tape blaring out. Then the music changed to Elvis singing 'It's Now or Never' so I guessed she and Jed had gone upstairs to her bedroom to discuss tactics.

4

After that I was filled with a sudden longing to see my real dad. I knew he wasn't being filled with a longing to see me. The only sudden longings my real dad had were to watch the latest round of the FA cup. He liked going to the pub too with some people he called 'the boys'. But I decided to go over just the same. I *knew* Blossom would appreciate a bit of help with Timmie and Petal. She hardly got any time to play with them since she started re-tiling the roof. And anyway, there was *some* good news. At least I was going to have a permanent baby to cuddle and not just sometimes ones like Timmie and Petal.

When I got over there the house was in darkness.

Blossom answered the door, a candle guttering romantically in her careworn hand.

'Charlie!' She gave me a hug. When I prised myself away from the sticky mess all down the front of her apron I heard my real dad call from in front of the TV.

'Blossom, haven't you changed that fuse yet?'

'It's Charlie,' she called.

'It's no good trying to blame other people,' I heard my

dad say. 'Hurry up, the Miss Exotic Mediterranean Wet T-Shirt contest from Margate starts on Eurogames in a minute.'

My real dad came out of the front room. When the smoke from his cigarette cleared, he saw me standing on the doorstep looking forlorn.

'Charlie! This is a nice surprise.'

'I told you it was her,' Blossom said.

'No you didn't.'

'Hi, Dad.' I put my arms up to hug him but he stepped neatly aside. I still got the whiff of hair grease and stale tobacco that always made me think of him. It's funny how smells remind you of people. Oil and aftershave always remind me of Al (she likes men's fragrances better than women's), Body Shop body-lotion and furniture polish make me think of Jed, chocolate and sausage meat remind me of Amy, and our teacher, Mr Donovan (Jason), always smells of stale beer and chalk. Gazza, of course, just smells like heaven.

'You've missed dinner again, Charlie,' my real dad was saying without a trace of regret, ' . . . but never mind, come on in.'

I kicked aside the pile of broken toys on the doorstep and went inside.

'Where's your school uniform, Charlie?' My real dad brushed the ash from the front of his shirt. Blossom ran to get the dustpan and brush. 'I paid good money for that.'

'Dad, that was three years ago. I've grown out of it.'

He tutted. 'That's the damn trouble with kids. Always growing.'

Talking about growing reminded me about the baby. Not that I'd really forgotten. How could you forget that most wonderful miracle of nature ever to be invented by man?

'Mum's having a baby,' I said.

I heard Blossom gasp from the cupboard under the

27

stairs. She crawled out backwards, clasping the packet of fuse wire and electrician's pliers to her apron. As she did so she tripped over the dustpan and brush she'd just dustpan and brushed the fag-ash up with. 'Quick,' she said, picking herself up and wiping the blood from her nose. 'Your dad's fainted.'

Upstairs, Petal began to cry.

'See to the baby, Blossom,' were my real dad's first coherent words.

Blossom ran upstairs, her little worn slippers pitty-pat patting on the bare boards.

'Well,' my real dad said later, recovering in the chair with his feet up on a stool and a hot water bottle clutched to his tobacco tin. 'That's a turn up for the book.'

'Oh, I don't know,' I said, sitting at his feet. (I'd read that it was wise always to be lower than your man. Apparently they feel very insecure if you tower above them. Even if it is only your real dad.) 'I thought Manchester United would win.'

'No, no, Charlie,' my real dad said, switching off the Euro-cup Winners Winner's Cup for half a second. 'Your mum, getting pregnant.'

I smiled. 'I know. It's wonderful, isn't it?'

'A miracle if you ask me.'

'Yes,' I said. I sighed and clasped my hands to my bosom. 'All babies are a miracle.'

'No, they're not.'

'I think Jed will make a very good father.' Blossom stood in the doorway trying to wipe Petal's sick off her sleeve with one end of the soiled disposable nappy.

'No, he won't,' my real dad glowered.

'Mum's not going to use disposables,' I piped up. 'She says they're environmentally unfriendly.'

'She would,' my real dad said. 'She thinks breathing pollutes the atmosphere.'

I giggled and went to hug him again. He really was so sweet. He was still sitting with his feet up so he couldn't move out of the way in time. 'Only if you're a man,' I assured him. 'And really, nine million disposable nappies rotting on garbage tips per day *is* rather a lot, Dad.'

'No, it's not,' he said. 'Load of rubbish.'

I went to take the baby from Blossom's arms. It was really hard for her to carry that bucket of disposables, a pile of ironing, Timmie's little death-truck that had been lying on the stairs, *and* baby-Petal all at once.

I cuddled Petal and kissed her chubby, milk-encrusted face. It smelt as if Blossom hadn't washed her bottom properly but I didn't say anything.

'Have you finished tiling the roof, Blossom?' I asked politely.

'Yes,' she sighed, pushing back her lack-lustre hair. I think the lumps of white stuff sticking in it must have been mortar. 'Thank goodness.'

I'd offered her my Ultra-glisten hair-setting foam on several occasions but she'd refused.

'Your father likes me to look natural,' she'd said, smiling wearily.

'Oh, it's all natural ingredients,' I'd insisted, looking at the list on the side of the bottle. 'Al won't use anything artificial . . . look . . . '

But the cod-liver oil, extract of dandelion, and chickweed hadn't convinced her.

'No, you haven't finished the roof at all,' my real dad said. 'You've got four more ridge tiles to put on.'

Blossom smiled sweetly. 'I'm going to get them from the builder's merchants tomorrow after I've dismantled the bookshelves, taken up the carpet, scrubbed the stairs, cleaned behind the cooker, and taken Timmie to nursery school.'

'Don't tell fibs,' my real dad said. 'Charlie will think you've got a lot to do. You know I promised to take up the carpet in the lavatory. All you've got to do is shampoo it first.'

29

'Taking up the carpet?' I asked, puzzled. It wasn't at all like my real dad to do anything so strenuous. Especially with that bad back he constantly reminded everyone about.

'Yes,' he said defensively. 'There's half an hour between the end of the men's downhill skiing and the racing from Newmarket. You don't expect me to sit here and do nothing do you, Charlie?'

'Yes,' I said. I tucked little Petal's soggy nappy back inside her sweet, darling off-white all-in-one Mothercare baby suit. I remember the suit had been Timmie's. It still had his Ribena stains down the front. 'Why do you need to take the carpet up in the loo anyway?' I asked. 'I quite like it.'

I remembered we'd had bare boards in our house for ages when Mum had been going through her SCABS (Stop the Countryside Allowing Bald Sheep) interlude. She'd said people should be perfectly content with floorboards when sheep's self-respect was at risk. My everlasting memory of that time was trying to sabotage sheep shearing equipment and only getting a hair-cut for my pains. Anyway, I thought Al looked great with the bandage round her head. Somehow it made her look . . . I don't know . . . feminine. Especially after all her friends at the Body Building Club wrote anti-male-farmer slogans on it. And I suppose the sheepdog's hair would have grown again quite quickly after Mum sheared it off.

'We're transferring it to Petal's bedroom,' my real dad said. He glared at Blossom. 'And when Blossom finds a job we'll perhaps be able to afford a new one for the loo. We've been married for five years and she hasn't found a job yet.'

'Oh, Dad.' I managed to get my Barry Manilow badge from Petal's tiny hand before she stuffed it into her mouth. I didn't think Barry would appreciate being stuffed into a baby's gullet. 'You are funny.'

'No, I'm not,' he said.

I was just about to tell them we were moving but at that moment all the lights went out again.

'For God's sake, Blossom,' I heard my dad say. 'Can't you even mend a bloody fuse properly?'

I think it was the cat Blossom tripped over on her way back to the cupboard under the stairs. It could have been the Hoover that was still lying on its side in the hallway although Hoovers don't usually yowl and screech and go belting up the stairs like bats (or cats) out of hell.

My real dad was obviously worried. 'And mind my golf clubs,' he yelled. 'I'm playing in a tournament next week.'

'Again . . . ?' Blossom protested weakly.

My real dad raised his bushy, nicotine-stained eyebrows to the ceiling. 'Honestly, Blossom,' he said, 'you know a man has to have his hobbies.' I could smell the angry smell of his cigarette smoke billowing towards us. When I'd given Petal the kiss of life I felt my way up to her nursery and popped her into her dear little cot. She lay here dribbling and burping at me and playing with the little fluffy vampire Al had sent her.

After she'd filled her nappy again she went off to sleep.

I didn't get much chance to say anything else. I sat in the front room with my real dad. He kept telling me to shut up so he could hear the snooker commentary and Blossom was up re-fitting the bathroom cupboard. That was after she'd rescued Timmie from the roof. He'd climbed out of the attic window. She just managed to stop him stuffing himself down the chimney pot. I thought playing Father Christmasses was a jolly good game but my real dad didn't think it too funny when a blast of soot came down the chimney and blotted out the TV screen.

Then Petal woke up again. She'd bruised her ear where her head had got stuck between the bars of the cot. I'm sure she didn't get any proper sleep anyway with Blossom hammering away in the bathroom. I don't actually think it was that that gave me a headache. It was probably my dad shouting upstairs for his supper that did it.

'I'll get it, Dad,' I called, taking the cotton wool out of my ears.

'What's the matter with Blossom? I didn't marry her to get my own supper, you know. Doesn't she realize I've been at work all day?'

Blossom appeared at the top of the stairs. I think it was an accident that a hammer fell from her carpenter's tool belt and almost knocked my dad out again. Luckily she managed to dodge out of the way, otherwise it would have cracked her head open when he threw it back up.

'Oh, dear,' Blossom sighed, wiping her weary brow. 'Glass is *so* expensive.'

'Never mind about that.' My real dad glanced back at the soot-stained TV. 'What about my supper? You can go to the glazier's first thing in the morning. It won't take five minutes to replace that pane. If you hadn't dropped the hammer in the first place I wouldn't have had to throw it back.' He winced and put his hand on his waist. 'And you know I've got a bad back.'

'Dad . . . ' I plucked irritatingly at the sleeve of his cardigan. 'I'll get your supper.'

'No, you won't,' my real dad said sweetly.

'I will,' I insisted sootily. 'What do you want? Beans on toast?'

'Eggs,' he said.

Later, when I got home, I noticed my face was covered in soot. It's OK dressing up as a coal miner for a fancy dress competition but you look pretty daft going around with black cheeks any other time. Especially if you're wearing bright purple, glossy-moisturized kiss-proof lipstick.

* * *

32

Before I knew it, it was time to go home. Jed was picking me up in his Creative Consultancy's BMW. Al had allowed him to bring it home for the weekend. We were going to load it up with stuff to take to our new shack.

I thought it was the car horn hooting outside the front gate although it could have been one of the neighbours yelling for my dad to turn down the telly.

'Bye, Blossom,' I called. I dried my hands and put away the last of the twenty-six dirty plates, fourteen baby bottles, fifty-nine beer glasses and seven dirty ashtrays that I had washed up. I heard the angry clump of my real dad's slippers on the stairs and guessed he'd gone to bed.

Blossom appeared again at the top of the landing. I think it was a hack-saw she was trying to prise from Timmie's sweet, sticky hand. I suppose it could have been the Stanley knife that I'd seen my real dad cleaning his toenails with in the front room earlier. Anyway, she managed to get three of the screws out of Timmie's mouth before she shouted goodbye.

'Come and see us again soon, Charlie,' she called in a sweet, exhausted voice.

I was just about to tell her we were moving to the country so I wouldn't see her for a while, when my real dad shouted from the bedroom.

'Can't you lot be a bit quieter — *some* people are trying to get to sleep. Some of us have to go to work in the morning, you know.'

Blossom smiled and held her weary finger to her lips.

Just then Petal woke up again and began to scream.

'Had a nice time, Charlie?' Jed asked as I got in the car. He gave me a hug.

'Yes, lovely, thanks. My real dad let me do the washing up and get his supper.'

'What *is* that down the front of your Oxford University

sweatshirt?' Jed stared at me and curled his lip. (I didn't think my sweatshirt could ever have actually belonged to someone who went to Oxford University. I mean, surely no one with any *brains* would have drawn pictures of bare men with marker pen all over the back? I'm surprised it hadn't been banned from the charity shop.)

'Oh . . . ' I brushed off the mess. 'Only Petal's dribble, I expect.'

Jed brushed Petal's dribble that had been transferred from my sweatshirt to his designer blazer when he hugged me. 'Oh, Charlie,' he said. He speeded up to twenty miles a hour. 'I'm so looking forward to having my own baby dribbling down my clothes.' His strong, granite-jawed face lit up with anticipation. I could see why my mum adored him so much. He was like a kind of New-Superman with a pony tail and portable phone. His little gold bell-shaped ear-ring tinkled merrily as he leaned forward to switch off his *Sound of Music* tape. 'I've just been to book in for my first ante-natal class,' he chirped proudly. The old lady we'd just almost bowled over on the pedestrian crossing picked herself up and shook her fist at us. I looked in the rear-view mirror and saw her hobble painfully up the steps to the Day Centre. I knew Jed shouldn't have been trying to thumb through a Mothercare catalogue and drive at the same time.

'Is Mum going?' I asked.

'What, to the old people's Day Centre?' Jed must have seen the old lady too. I didn't actually know why she was going into the *Day* Centre when it was ten o'clock at night. Maybe there was an all-night Rave going on, or basket-weaving classes or something.

'No, Jed,' I said patiently, 'to ante-natal classes.'

'No, she's got Tae Kwon Do on Thursdays. She'll try to fit one or two in I expect but what with organizing the school panto, assertiveness classes, motor cycle maintenance, embroidery, *and* tap dancing I can see she's hardly going to have the time.'

'What about the band?'

'What band?' Jed glanced in the mirror. 'My hair hasn't come loose has it?' He reached back to make sure his pony tail wasn't coming adrift.

'No, Jed. Not your elastic band. The all-singing, all-dancing, all-girl heavy metal band Al plays in — you know, Deathshead Condom.'

Jed shrugged. 'Oh, she won't give that up — at least not until she's too pregnant to fit on stage with her double-bass.' Jed tossed his Mothercare catalogue into the back seat and fiddled with the radio. 'God,' he said, 'I'm hungry. I really fancy a pilchard and peanut butter sundae. How about you, Charlie?'

'No thanks,' I said.

Jed sighed. 'It's being pregnant, Charlie. You get weird cravings for things.'

'What, like my mum?'

'Now, Charlie . . . you mustn't call your mother weird.'

'No, Jed. Pregnant like . . . oh, forget it!'

I sat back in the seat, enjoying the luxury. Mind you, anything beats being crammed on the back of Mum's Kawasaki with Jed and the double-bass any day. Jed had found Radio One and was trying to hum along with the latest disco-funk-rave hit.

'I'll come to ante-natal classes with you, Jed,' I said.

I could think of nothing more wonderful than being surrounded by bow-fronted ladies in sweet, floral maternity smocks and expressions of contentment and morning sickness.

'It's my dream to have a baby — as well as being an actor, of course.' I held out my feet and wiggled my Reeboks. 'I could do with a new pair of shoes as well.'

'Me too,' Jed sighed.

'Yours are OK.' I looked down at his Gucci loafers.

'No, Charlie,' Jed gave me a new-man smile.

'Oh . . . you mean you want to be an actor.' I could just imagine him playing the part of Hannibal the Cannibal.

Jed smiled again and swerved to miss a policeman on a bike. He really should have had some lights on it at that time of night. Jed patted my bony knee affectionately.

'No, Charlie, I mean it's always been my dream to have a baby. But there you go, Charlie, we men can't win 'em all.' He burped and patted his stomach. 'Oh dear,' he said. 'I've got heartburn.'

5

The next night we went to the school for a panto meeting.

Al roared up in a hail of Kawasaki smoke and motor-bike boots. I came in Jed's BMW. There hadn't been room on the bike since Mum started to grow her heavenly bump. She said *four* people and her double-bass was pushing it a bit. Al clutched the new script to her smock. She'd told me she'd taken five minutes of her lunch break to re-write the whole thing.

'On re-cycled paper, of course, Charlie,' she'd yelled as she whizzed along beside us up the by-pass. I saw she'd written 'Sexist Pantomimes Immediately Terminated' on the front of her helmet. She leaned from the saddle to give Jed a kiss. He blushed and waved coyly to the police car whizzing up behind, sirens screaming, blue light going like the clappers. Al roared through the orange traffic light and was soon a black, pregnant speck in the distance. I don't think the police car ever did catch her. Certainly when we saw it, it was upside-down on the central reservation. They'd never overtake her going along on their roof.

All the cast had turned up. I felt sure some of them had other things to do but it was probably the threatening phone calls that persuaded them. I suppose if Al hadn't got her friends from the battered wives refuge to make the calls they might have ignored them.

Even Mr Donovan had dragged himself out of the Duck and Shotgun. Sonia Scissorhands greeted my mum with a bouquet of flowers and a click of her fingernails. I don't think Al noticed she'd accidentally sliced the blossoms off in a moment of stage-fright.

'Thanks,' Mum said, sniffing the stalks.

When Gazza had finished kicking the ball around the back of the hall I went to give him a hug.

'I wish I was playing Snow White,' I sighed against his shin pad. (He was actually lying on the floor at the time. He'd just been knocked over by Sammy's wheelchair. Sammy was trying to break his record of fifty times round the hall in five minutes.)

I got down to Gazza's level to talk to him. I knew that wasn't really what you were supposed to do. I'd heard my mum on the phone to her friend Fiona lots of times. 'Now don't you sink to his level, Fi,' she'd say, shouting above the laughing of Fiona's new pet hyena. 'Just because he won't let you go off to Majorca for a fortnight with the milkman, don't try to stop him spending a weekend with his secretary.'

And she certainly *never* sunk to Jed's level. She was at least six inches taller than him and that's *after* she'd had her head shaved. Mind you, I did see her kneel down once to help him unravel his ball of wool from the spokes of the Kawasaki. I knew he shouldn't be knitting those baby clothes while haring up the motorway at ninety.

Seeing we were all assembled Mum leapt on to the stage.

Jed stepped forward in consternation.

'Sweetie, you shouldn't be jumping around like that.'

Mum patted his head. 'It's all right, hunky,' she said. 'Having a baby is a perfectly natural thing. No reason to change our behaviour at all.' Jed blushed and smiled at her words.

'OK, you guys,' she shouted assertively. 'Here's what's going to happen.'

'Why shouldn't your mum jump around,' Mary Hadda asked. 'Has she had her hair done?' She was peering into one of Jed's Next shiny blazer buttons trying to adjust her bra strap.

'She's having a baby, Miss Lamb,' I said. 'I told you.'

Mary looked vague. 'Did you?' she said, examining her complexion in Jed's top button. 'I never listen to you kids.' She took an aerosol can from her vanity case and sprayed her hair. I didn't really think Jed wanted hair lacquer all over the front of his scarlet and kingfisher satin waistcoat but he didn't say anything. He didn't even ask her if it was ozone friendly. He was too busy gazing up adoringly at my mum. I didn't actually think the stage would stand her weight but it seemed to be OK. As long as she didn't start stomping, or head-banging or anything and there was no danger of that as long as no one put Status Quo in the tape machine.

And that was impossible because it had been pinched along with the grand piano yonks ago.

Sonia put up her fingernails. 'Er . . . Ms Scroggins,' she stammered. '*I'm* actually the drama mistress.' I noticed for the first time that she was wearing the most deliciously heavenly pair of high-heeled navy and white spotted shoes I have ever seen in my entire life. (Sonia, not my mum. *She'd* never wear a pair of deliciously spotted anything.) They were just like the ones Julie Andrews wore in *The Sound of Music* . . . or was it Joan Collins in *Dynasty*? I couldn't quite remember. Anyway, they were absolutely magic. I made a vow there and then to pop off to the charity shop on Saturday to see if they'd got any the same. I supposed I could always get a plain pair and get Jed to paint some polka-dots on with his creative paints. It wouldn't be quite the same but charity shoppers can't be choosers.

'*Mistress!*' Al was thundering. 'Don't talk to me of mistresses. How women can allow themselves — '

'No, Mum,' I interrupted, beckoning to everyone to come back into the hall. 'Our drama *teacher*.'

'Oh . . .' If she had been anyone else she would have looked pregnantly abashed. As it was she just looked pregnant. I wasn't sure but it looked as if she'd stuffed a cushion up her smock but when she lifted it up I saw she'd filled her bum bag with copies of her new version of *Snow White*. 'Well, that's OK, then,' she said. 'Right, let's get started. Sonia . . . ' Sonia came back warily. 'I'll be happy to listen to your advice as long as there's not too much of it.'

As it turned out, Sonia didn't have any advice for Al to ignore.

First of all she accidentally caught one of her nails in Jed's ear-ring while quoting 'Is that a dagger I see before me?'

Sammy almost fell out of his wheelchair laughing.

Then, during one of Mum's demonstrations of Snow White defending herself from sexual harassment by the prince, she accidentally knocked Sonia's Juliet wig off with her heavy-duty chain. At this point Paddy woke up and shouted, 'Put the boot in, missis.'

Al's look of contempt was like the kind of sneer Dracula gives someone when he's about to bite their neck.

'*Mrs!*' she shouted.

Paddy hid behind his beer-crate, although as he popped up to see if the coast was clear Al lifted up her smock, wrenched off her bum bag and chucked it at him. It hit him on the nut. I think she must have had her Swiss Army knife inside because it almost knocked him for six. I wondered if Gazza might rush over to play soccer with it but he didn't. In fact Gazza didn't rush anywhere. He was sitting in the corner filling in his Pools coupon.

'And you *know* I don't believe in any kind of violence, Paddy,' Al shouted. 'Even when provoked.'

'Pardon?' Wanda stopped dancing and spoke for the first time.

'I'm not talking to you,' Al said gently. 'I'M TALKING TO PADDY!'

'Pardon?' Wanda said again, looking confused. She fumbled in her rucksack for another tape.

The thing was, of course, that no one had realized she was bald underneath. Not Al underneath her smock, or Wanda underneath her earphones, but Sonia underneath her Juliet wig. When she had finished crying all her greasepaint had come off so she had to go home. I watched her teetering unsteadily out of the doors in those fab shoes. She obviously *did* care even though she was muttering 'Frankly, my dear, I don't give a damn.' I don't think she realized it was Paddy's shoulder she was crying on. I'm sure she would have had her handkerchief over her nose, not dabbing her greasepaint-less cheeks, if she had. And I'm sure if she hadn't been so blinded by her tears she would have stopped him using her Juliet wig to carry his lager cans in. The last thing we saw was Sonia balanced precariously on Paddy's crossbar clutching on to his shredded denim jacket with her fingernails. They left a trail of what looked like lager behind them. She had obviously opened a couple of tins by mistake.

Anyway . . . the new cast list was:

Snow White — Amy
The Prince — Gazza
The Evil StepFATHER — Sharon Smith
Snow White's Dear Mother — Paddy Powell
The Woodcutter — Sammy
The Policeperson — Ms Al Scroggins (plain clothes — she says uniforms are a symbol of power and domination [male])

41

Seven Small Persons —
Mick-the-Dick
Mr Donovan (Jason) (on his knees in his Father Christmas outfit)
Wanda Walkman (that's if she heard)
Mary Hadda (without her high heels)
Ms Keegan in a beard (no one else wanted the part)
Mrs Wally the Cleaner (she just happened to be sweeping the corridor and got roped in)
A Mystery Star Guest (whose identity Al wouldn't reveal).

I did actually wonder if it might be Terry Wogan as Mum was on his show once, although he wouldn't be playing a small person, would he? And she'd said it was discriminating against adults if only kids were allowed to take part.

This is my mum's version of her Panto without Sexism.

SNOW WHITE AND THE SEVEN SMALL PERSONS

SCENE 1 — Interior day

Snow White's Evil Step-Dad's looking in the mirror.
    'Mirror, Mirror by the bed.
    Am I better looking than Jed?'
When the mirror pipes up 'No he isn't and he'd better watch it because Snow White's got a new bloke who's not only a new man but he does the washing up, goes to Tesco's and is hunky to boot,' Snow White's Evil Step-Dad goes bananas. Then Sharon (the ES-D) orders the Woodperson (Sammy) to run S.W. over, then hide the body. The Woodperson says he's not ruining his tyres for some crummy Evil Step-Dad and lets S.W. scarper.
    She finds this little cottage. (It sounded just like the one

me and Gazza dream of. Well . . . me anyway. Gazza would live anywhere as long as there was a football pitch near and you don't get many of those in the middle of a wood, do you?)

When the Seven Small Persons get home S.W. strikes a bargain. *She* won't tell the Council they're living in a wood without planning permission and threatening the Queendom's rural heritage if they do the housework while she works down the mine. After half a micro-second's argument the Small Persons agree.

When the Evil Step-Dad looks in the mirror again he says:

'Mirror, mirror, don't have a fit.
At last old Snow White has snuffed it.'

And the mirror replies:

'Oh no, she ain't, you silly old twit,
She's working down the small person's pit.'

With that the Evil Step-Dad goes bananas again. He puts on this Dame Edna outfit so no one will think he looks weird and goes off to find Snow White. He mugs her on her way home from work. When the Seven Small Persons find her, they stuff her into this glass coffin and put her in a clearing in the woods. Then this Prince comes along for a picnic. (My mum's a Hunt Saboteur so he couldn't be out hunting . . . any violence would have spoiled the whole thing.) She *was* going to have him picking flowers but said that we'll lose all our indigenous wild flora if everyone goes about picking bluebells and primroses and stuff.

Anyway, this Prince sees Snow White and falls in love with her. He bribes the Small Persons to let him have the coffin then, like a twit, drops it and Snow White tumbles out. When the Prince tries to pick her up, she awakes and accuses the Prince of sexual harassment. (I tried to get

43

this changed. I *know* Gazza would *never* sexually harass anyone. After all, I've given him enough chances. And he'd never be able to get her Princess's boob-tube off anyway, not without a crowbar.)

Anyway, this Prince manages to convince her he was only trying to pick her up and she takes him off to her Kindly Mother's castle to live equally ever after. The Evil Step-Dad's arrested and goes down for seven years for attempted murder.

Jed was to be artistic director, Sonia Scissorhands in charge of wardrobe (I could see everyone would be dressed in ribbons), Ms Keegan (as well as playing a bearded Small Person) could arrange a Keep-Fit class so the actors were in tip-top top-to-toe shape, Mr Donovan (Jason) was to be in charge of refreshments (liquid) as well as playing a Small Person on his knees. Amy said she wanted that job instead of the starring role, but Mum asserted herself and smacked Amy neatly on the chins. Mary Hadda was to be allowed to take off her beard to do everyone's make-up. I was to be Snow White's understudy and publicity person. I didn't think being Amy's understudy would actually take me on the road to stardom but I suppose you had to start somewhere. All I hoped was that Amy wasn't too heavy for the stage. If she was then she'd be going *through* the boards instead of *treading* the boards. And *me* as her *under*study would be squashed flat.

'And we'll give a performance for the Old Folk,' Mum said at the end of the meeting. She shoved Jed off her lap. 'They need something to brighten their lives. Especially the women.'

'They have a great time, Mum,' I said. 'I saw them rock 'n' rolling at the Day Centre only last Sunday morning.'

'The women don't,' Mum said, donning her helmet ready for the race home. 'After a lifetime of drudgery they need cheering up. That reminds me . . . ' she turned to Jed. 'Have you finished packing our stuff?'

Jed sighed. 'Yes, sweetie, all done. It's ruined my hands.' He took out his jar of Super-soft hand cream and put a blob on his palm.

Al hugged him. 'Don't worry, darling, all that country air we'll be breathing in will cure you of everything.' She wiped Super-soft off her neck.

'Even my morning sickness?' Jed looked forlorn.

'Yes, sweetness.' Al patted his stomach in an almost-maternal gesture.

I turned to Gazza and made a vomiting kind of face. He looked at me indifferently over the top of his soccer magazine.

'Feel sick, Charlie?' He jumped up. 'Oh, you poor thing. I'm off.'

The last I saw of him he was shooting off home on his bike. I thought at first he'd got a boil on his back but realized afterwards he'd shoved his football up his jumper. Even if he had got a boil on his back I wouldn't care. I'd love him if he had boils everywhere.

'We're off, Charlie,' Mum said, attaching a tow-rope to the back of the bike. 'If Sammy's mum turns up, I've taken him home. I'm stopping off at the garage to get some lead-free on the way back, so don't worry if I'm late.'

'Cheerio, you lot,' Sammy said, putting on his helmet.'Hi-ho, Silver!' He pretended to crack a whip as Mum revved up the Kawasaki. The last thing we saw was Sammy's arm waving at us as they shot up the road.

When we'd woken Jason from his alcoholic daze, picked Jed up off the floor (he'd got stuck doing his relaxation exercises), and called Ms Keegan away from the Jane Fonda video, we stuffed all Amy's food wrappers into the bin. I knew Jed shouldn't have offered her a lift home. It took three-quarters of an hour to prise her out through the car door. I said she shouldn't have eaten those eighteen treacle-filled Scrummy Do-nuts on the way back to her house. We'd managed to push her *into* the car without any trouble at all.

By the time we got back Al was fast asleep. At least I think it was her I could hear snoring upstairs. It could have been thunder, I suppose.

6

I've decided to write to my *Real Love* magazine's Agony Uncle for advice. Here's what I put:

Dear Billy Brokenheart,
I'm almost fourteen and have two ambitions — one to be a wife and mother (if that counts as two, then I've got three ambitions, not two). The second (or third) one is to be an actor. (I wouldn't mind a pair of spotty shoes too but it's not crucial.) I'm in love with gorgeous Gaz. I've said I want us to feature together in the drama of life. A little cottage with a little mortgage. Lots of babies, lots of sleepless nights and shirts to iron. Maybe a Hollywood box office blockbuster with Tom Cruise. But the only star in Gazza's life is football. Where am I going wrong?
Love,
Charlie Scroggins.
P.S. My mum, her New-Man, and me are all green.

This is what Billy wrote back:

Dear Charlie,
It is quite acceptable these days, Charlie, for people of

the same sex to have a meaningful relationship but you must realize that being a wife and mother is probably not an option in your case. Starring roles — yes, Charlie. Motherhood . . . ? Well, medical science is progressing all the time, Charlie, so don't give up hope entirely.

The colour of your skin, whether green or otherwise, is not relevant. Why not apply to the BBC (Budding actor's Benevolent Club)? You also have to face the fact, Charlie, that some people like football better than anything. There are some things in life you cannot change. The main thing is to 'think positive'. I'm sure many of our readers will identify with your predicament and sympathize deeply, Charlie. Handle the situation with honesty and, Charlie, count your blessings. Remember, even people who have relationships with the *opposite* sex have problems so you'll never walk alone.

Charlie, I hope to see your name in lights.

Yours in agony,

Billy Brokenheart.

I thought at first Billy Brokenheart could not possibly be a real person but his photo was in the mag. so he must be. I mean, who with any *brain* would think Gaz was a girl. So I decided to ignore his advice. That's the great thing about asking people's advice, you can always ignore it.

On Saturday we moved.

Mum hired a truck, hi-jacked some of her friends from the Body Building Club and in no time at all our stuff was on the lorry. I think it must have been used to take cows to market because everything was covered in cows' pooh when we arrived in Pratt's Bottom.

Poor Jed had to wash himself in the old tin bath full of water someone had left outside the back door. Al did her nut. She said anyone who washed themselves in acid rain was asking for trouble. Poor Jed, the acid certainly hadn't done much for his hairstyle and where he'd splashed it over his feet, his white designer espadrilles would never be the same again. Al assured him we'd soon have running water. In fact, two seconds after her assertive phone call, the Water Board came round to connect it.

The Water Board official I thought I saw using Al's trampoline behind the hedge was in fact being used as a dumb-bell by one of Al's friends. There was certainly nothing dumb about him though, he was yelling like mad.

'That's the thing about body building,' my mum said, flexing her forearm. 'You've always got to be in training.'

Living in the country's not much different to living in the town. Except . . .

- a) You have to go on the bus to school.
- b) You can hear the roar of cows and sheep instead of the roar of traffic.
- c) You have to wear green wellies — even with your best second-hand designer rags.
- d) There's no shopping-mall to hang around in.
- e) Your mum goes greener.
- f) The farmer up the road drops pooh outside your gate when he's muck spreading.

Or at least he would if we *had* a gate. New-Man Jed said there used to be one but some drunken yobs from the Olde Worlde tranquille village pubbe wrenched it off its hinges and threw it into the slurry pit. Jed tried to get it out but certainly didn't come up smelling of flowers. That was strange because I'd heard my real dad say once, 'That bloke of hers could fall in a cess pit and come up smelling of roses.'

I was sitting in my new bedroom. Well . . . it's not exactly *new*. It's more like a hundred years old. You can tell that by the way the ceiling slopes. Still, there's plenty of room for the birds to nest in the gap where it's supposed to join the wall. Al says it'll be fine when she gets the window glazed — meanwhile an environmentally friendly biodegradable bin-bag pinned across the hole is perfectly OK.

There were lots of dramatically important things whirling around in my teenage brain. Which of my jumpers made my boobs look biggest? It was really hard to see *anything* with a black bag across the window, but I'd tried the red one with a picture of Batman in sequins on the front. It looked OK but Batman's ears covered the place where my boobs were supposed to be. Then I tried the pale blue angora one Blossom had knitted me. I think she must have been mowing the lawn at the time because there was grass growing in between the stitches.

My yellow sweatshirt looked best. I guessed it was because the words 'Princess Anne Does It On Horseback' were printed in bright orange letters across the front. I adore anything to do with the Royal Family. Wearing it made me feel kind of . . . patriotic. The words stuck out and so did everything else. Well . . . a little bit.

Another thing I was wondering was . . . when was I going to get that first kiss from my angel? Would seeing me in the sweatshirt prompt Fab Gazza into giving it to me? (The kiss not the sweatshirt.) I'd dreamed about it so often. Again, the kiss. I'd actually had nightmares about the sweatshirt. I think that was because the jagged hole in the back and the rust coloured stains that surrounded it looked totally sinister. When she brought it home, Al said I was imagining things. She'd found it in the gutter outside the House of Horrors and it had probably belonged to one of the attendants. Maybe that first kiss would be Gazza's Christmas present? I made a mental note to hang mistletoe absolutely everywhere so he'd have no excuse.

Amy said I was becoming obsessed about kissing Gazza and being obsessed about things definitely wasn't healthy. We were sitting against the wall in the playground when she said it.

'Honestly, Charlie, all you think about is sex,' she'd said, undoing the buttons of her mini-skirt.

'No, I don't,' I'd protested. 'It's just that when you're in love you naturally want to *make* love. Don't you remember our Personal Development classes?'

'Hmmph,' Amy stuffed two bananas into her mouth. Two seconds later she said, 'All I remember is that they went on too long — we were late for dinner once.'

'That's because Mary brought in her sports car boyfriend to give us a demo.'

Amy looked horrified. 'Not another demo, not your mum again?'

'No, Amy . . . Mary and her bloke.'

'Coke? Oh . . . yes please.'

I sighed. What was the use of having a best friend if she wasn't interested in your problems? I suppose she was too tied up with playing Snow White. Al had told me only that morning they'd managed to rent-a-tent to make Amy's costume from.

I left Amy trying to get up. I was sure I'd seen Gazza round the back of the boiler room but when I got there it was only Sharon Smith changing her clothes for the fifteenth time that day.

'Seen much of Gazza lately?' she asked.

I nodded. 'Quite a bit.'

She smirked and pulled up her turquoise and pink knee-socks. Then she tried to pull down her cabbage-coloured micro-skirt so at least it covered her purple knickers. 'Not as much as me, I bet.'

Well, she does live on the same estate as him so she would see a lot of him, wouldn't she? I knew he passed

51

her house on his bike every morning on his way to school. He often said, 'Sharon was just getting dressed this morning when I dawdled past.'

When I'd idly flipped through my *Just 13* mag. during French that day I'd found an article that told me how to do it. Not dawdle past Sharon Smith's house, I mean you've got to be a sex maniac to do that every day. How to get that first kiss, I mean. The name of the article that was about to reveal all was 'Seven Tips for a Sexy Snog'. It could be the answer to my prayers.

1) Soft music . . . (probably the Manchester United team singing their song for peace — Death to All who Oppose Us).
2) A full stomach . . . (I'd just have cooked sweet Gaz vegi-burgers with pink Angel Delight to follow) . . .
3) Good wine (I could pinch some of Jed's Designer Beaujolais if I could find it amongst all the stuff yet to be unpacked).
4) Perfume . . . (I still had some left from the bottle I got at the tombola last year. It was at the Hell's Angels' Tea Dance Al got involved in. It cost me five quid to find a winning ticket and I could have bought the scent at Tesco's for a pound.)
5) Number 5 was taking a scented bath together, but we didn't have a bath in our new shack so this didn't apply. I suppose we could dunk ourselves in the cattle trough but personally I didn't fancy it. Especially on a winter's night that was cold enough to freeze the lead in Jed's gold Filofax pencil.

I decided that instead of Number 5, I could read my gorgeous hunk some of the Erotic Poetry I'd copied out from a library book. Maybe some of the bits . . .'tasting the exotic flavours of her body' and 'playing the sensual game of love' might spur him on. Mind you, he'd prob-

52

ably think the game was football and spurring him on was something to do with Tottenham.

6) Soft lights. (This was definitely OK. A dustbin sack over your window's just the job.)

7) Whisper sexy promises. (I could just imagine myself whispering 'Gazza, kiss me and I'll let you score a goal. Give me a duster and I'll polish your glasses. Put your lips on mine and there won't be any penalties.')

If none of these worked I could always read my Judy Blume book again . . .

I turned to the back page of my mag. to read my stars.

'Three important planets are moving into your sphere,' it said. 'A starring role could come your way.'

Maybe I *would* get to play Snow White to Gazza's prince after all.

'Your health will be a star in the firmament.'

I wasn't sure what a firmament was but I wondered if it was the name of a breast-developing cream. I'd have to ask Al's friend Rosa — she knew about magic potions and stuff (and she worked in the Body Shop while her fourteen kids were at school). Actually I hoped that meant the large spot on the end of my nose would go away before the panto. It had shone like a star for ages. Even if I was only Amy's understudy, having a spotty nose is hardly the thing, is it?

I'd done a good job with publicity though. I'd put up notices in the Old Folks Day Centre, the Traditional Theatre Club Headquarters, the Battered Wives Refuge, the Body Building Club, the new Civic Centre (The Mayor was an old friend of my mum's. They were on a demo together once.), the Police Station. (I thought the local coppers would be interested as there was a police-person in the panto. Even if my mum was playing the part.) I'd tried to creep into the local Boy's Brigade HQ but Al had spotted me.

She had torn up the poster. 'We want no male-dominated fascist institutions at our performance,' she'd said.

Horoscope Horace also said:

'Star wars will be a feature of your future.'

I'd seen the film loads of times so he couldn't have meant that.

Downstairs I could hear Jed trying to sweep the leaves from the front room. He must have had Des O'Connor on again because his mobile phone was going like mad and no one was answering it.

I came down to see Mum come in waving her sledgehammer. It only made a *small* hole in the floorboards as she let it drop. I'd known they were rotten when the heel of my tatty black stilettos went through them whilst I was practising my relaxation exercise on the floor with Jed. Still, I don't suppose any mother *really* in labour would be doing it on the floor. Or in stiletto shoes for that matter.

Mum took off her lung-protector mask (she said the air was full of pesticides and would be until she persuaded our neighbouring farmer to go organic) and answered the phone. Her face wasn't so much flushed with the joy of expected motherhood as scarlet with rage as she listened for half a second to what the caller was saying.

'What!'

I dodged out of the way as she clutched a handful of crew cut. Her Guns'n'Rose-coloured fingernails only just missed my nose. Still, they might have knocked the spot off. Maybe I should stand a bit closer to Sonia at our panto rehearsals? Paddy Powell was always on about 'knocking things off' and now I knew what he was on about.

Al slammed down the phone. When she'd prised it from between the floorboards she shouted to Jed.

'Jed! Jed!' He came in from the kitchen where he'd gone to start the dinner. I suppose his face was black because the paraffin stove had blown up again. I knew it exploded yesterday because the organic lentil pie with wholemeal-crust pastry and free-range chicken-flavoured gravy had tasted like a bonfire. He wrung his hands into his apron.

'What is it, sweetie?' he said in alarm. 'Is it coming?'

'Armageddon, yes,' she shouted.

'That's a funny name for a baby,' I piped up, trying to hide my *Pash-Mag.* under the waistband of my emerald green velvet ski-pants. I'd brought it down to show Jed an article on 'Fabulous Sexmas Party Gear for New Men'.

Mum's look of disdain was beautiful to behold.

'No, not the baby,' she said hotly. 'The day of reckoning.'

'What . . .?' Jed was still confused. A lock of his hair had come out of its elastic band and covered one eye. I think it was a beetle that crawled up it but I'm not sure. That's one of the joys of living in the country, you are at one with nature. Or so Al had said as she hacked her way through the garden to the outside loo. 'It's not due until the 19th,' he went on.

'No . . . not *that* day,' Mum spluttered. (I knew she'd had a job reckoning exactly when the baby was due. They'd decided on the nineteenth because that was exactly nine months after Jed had started a new course of Super-virile Vitamin Pills Rosa had concocted from natural organic herbs and hormone tablets she'd pinched from her ex-husband's medicine cupboard. Her ex-husband had been a witch-doctor before he met Rosa. Now he was doing time for illegally removing the vocal chords of an opera singer who'd lived next door.)

'What then?' Jed said timidly.

'THAT . . .' she stormed, trying to extract her fist from the wall where she'd punched a hole in the wattle and daub with rage, '. . . was the organizer of a campaign to restore Snow White to her former self. Jed . . . Charlie . . . we have a new campaign after all.'

Jed threw me a glance of horror. The colour drained from his paraffin stove-flushed complexion. His expression turned to one of enthusiasm and unbridled delight (according to my *Pash-Mag*. 'unbridled delight' is what happens when you're with the one you love not, as I'd first thought, fun whilst riding horses without reins), when he saw Al chuck him a gorgon-glance.

'Who . . .?' he spluttered, wiping the grime from his cheek. 'What . . .?'

'Them . . .' Al threw a look of contempt at Jed's mobile phone. I almost expected it to shrivel up and turn to dust like Dracula does when someone drives a stake through his heart. 'The DIPPOS!'

'What?' I said, puzzled. 'What's it got to do with Sharon Smith?'

'Everything,' Al said. She took her combat gear from the tea-chest and stripped off her carpenter's smock. 'It has to do with any one of our starring cast.'

'Yes . . . but who are the DIPPOS?' Jed asked tremulously.

'Dramatists Insisting on Proper Pantomime Organization and Structure.' Al tried to pull her camouflage jacket down over her bump. 'They're an off-shoot of the Traditional Theatre lot. Branched out on their own, some twit said.' She took a deep breath and held it. Luckily the jacket went over her bump that time or else she'd have been in trouble. The jacket was a bit small under normal circumstances. Especially since she'd been body building. But to have a *baby* sticking out between the buttons would look totally ridiculous. 'So . . . ' she donned her helmet and picked up her axe. 'It's war after all, my darlings. Jed, forget about your morning sickness . . . this will be your best performance yet.'

7

We didn't see much of the DIPPOS while we were rehearsing S.W. and the S.S.Ps. Just a few stragglers traditionally waving banners. I think it must have been Al's friends that kept them away. I mean, who wants to try and disrupt panto rehearsals with a dozen Body Builders and several Black Belt Karate people standing outside?

Still, Rosa often came along to entertain everyone with a few calypsos and a bit of limbo dancing whilst they hung around the corridors. At least they weren't bored. I'm sure it wasn't them who vandalized the canteen looking for high-protein food.

One Body Builder tried to practise limbo dancing under the loo door. She was only discovered by Mrs Wally the cleaner the next morning. She'd called to Mary Hadda to help her get the Body Builder out.

Mary had thrown up her soft-as-your-face manicured hands in horror.

'I'm not going into the boys' toilets, Mrs Wally. I might get my dress dirty.' She'd smoothed down the layers of her mustard-colour chiffon skirt in distress.

I was pushing Sammy past at the time.

'Go on, Miss,' Sammy said, grinning. 'There won't be

anyone in there yet. They've all had their fags on the way to school.' He bounced his basket-ball off the wall.

'Wass goin' on?' Mr Donovan reeled towards us.

'Some Body Builder's stuck under the loo door, Sir,' Sammy piped up.

'Oh, is that all?' Jason put his hand to his forehead. 'It's not Arnold Schwarzen . . . thingy . . . is it?'

Sammy laughed. 'Don't be daft, Sir. You drunk? What would Arnie Schwarzenegger be doing at our school? Not exactly Hollywood, is it?'

'I really don't know.' Jason frowned. 'Ouch . . . Don't keep bouncing that ball, Samuelson, I've got a headache.'

'Sorry, Sir.' Sammy grinned again and put the ball on his lap. 'Oh well, I'm off.' He shot away. The last thing I saw he was trying to beat Amy to the classroom. If she got stuck in the doorway again, he'd never get through.

'Well.' Mrs Wally shook her trolley in anger. Her diamanté ear-rings tinkled like a chandelier in the wind. 'What are we going to do? I'm not going in there. How can I mop the floor with some bleedin' Body Builder stuck under the bleedin' door?' She tilted her baseball cap to the back of her head and scratched her scalp. The charms on her 22-carat gold charm bracelet tinkled like sleigh bells. I think the white flakes that drifted out of her hair could have been bathroom cleaner but I suppose they might have been dandruff.

'Oh dear,' Mary took her little mirror from her vanity case and examined her teeth for lipstick. 'The Body Builder's not injured, surely? I can't stand the sight of blood.'

'Neither can I,' Jason said. 'Especially after a night out.' He staggered away. Mary had already gone to do her hair ready for lessons. Luckily Paddy came past. When we told him what was up, he went inside the loos.

'I'll just put the boot in,' we heard him muttering. Then there was a scream and the Body Builder came out holding Paddy up by the scruff of the ear-ring.

'I didn't mean to kick you there,' he sobbed. 'Look, mate, take some of me lager.' He struggled to take a can from his pocket.

'Lager?' The Body Builder flexed her muscles at us. 'Don't touch the stuff. Milk, high-protein vitamin drinks, mineral water, Horlicks, fruit juice . . . four sets, fourteen repetitions of each . . . '

'Never 'eard of it,' Paddy said.

The last thing we saw was the Body B. doing arm curls and Paddy yelling for her to stop.

'Are you feeling nervous, hunky?' My mum asked Jed a few days before the dress rehearsal. We were having supper by candlelight. She swiped at a moth fluttering to its death around the flame and gave Jed a hug.

When he got his breath back, he said, 'Ohh, yes.' He sighed tremulously. 'I'll be glad when it's over now. I've had such backache . . . even my relaxation exercises don't help much.'

'You're not even in it,' I said. I waved my hands in the air to dry my super-dooper Red-for-Danger, one-coat gloss. Even then a dried leaf stuck to my little fingernail. It was *really* annoying.

'No, Charlie . . . I meant nervous about having the baby. It is Jed's first, you know.' Al took a swig of cod-liver oil and popped several Vitamin Mother-to-Be tablets into her mouth. She washed them down with a mouthful of calcium-enriched blackcurrant health drink.

'Oh . . . ' My heart hip-hopped excitedly when I thought about the baby's arrival. Even though the three little jackets I'd knitted hadn't turned out very well, I supposed they could always do as nappies, or floor cloths. Mind you, I've never seen purple and crimson striped nappies (or floor cloths for that matter). I wasn't actually fond of that colour combination. Jed had been getting *Historical Home* magazine since we moved and no one had those colours anywhere. Especially not on their babies. Still, I knew Mum hated gender stereotyping so blue and pink were definitely out.

Over the previous week, Al had been making a cradle in the kitchen. I'd thought it was for the Werewolf Chapter of the Hell's Angels' nativity play but I was wrong as usual. I thought all the mud would come off it if we scrubbed really hard. I said the baby would be just as well off in an orange box but Al said it *was* an orange box. It's just that she had draped it with black curtain material she'd got when the funeral parlour had put its old ones out for the bin men.

The day she finished the cradle I arrived back from tea at my real dad's. Blossom had sent over a parcel of baby clothes that Petal had outgrown.

'What's this crap?' Al said when I turned up with them.

I hurriedly wiped the remains of sausage, mash, beans, chips, and Mother's Pride spread with high cholesterol Anchor from around my mouth.

'Er . . . Blossom didn't have any health food in the cupboard,' I stammered.

Al scowled. 'No . . . that . . . ' She pointed to the parcel under my arm. I glanced down at the centre page of my real dad's *Bimbo* magazine Blossom had inadvertently wrapped the stuff in.

'Er . . . it's a photograph of someone,' I said.

Al scowled again. 'No . . . what's in the parcel, Charlie?'

'Oh . . . it's from Blossom. Clothes for the baby.'

'What . . . paid for by your father?' she shouted, tossing the parcel in the dustbin. She'd just had another run-in with the farmer and was wiping the blood off her hands. Al had lain down in front of the farmer's JCB to try to stop him grubbing out one of his hedges. He was furious because she bent the bucket but the hospital said his arm wasn't broken too badly and the cut on his leg would mend in no time with a dozen or so stitches.

Jed said he didn't know *who* would milk the cows while the farmer was in hospital. Mum suggested he did it but Jed had gone quite pale under his all-natural, stay-a-week non-allergic fake tan and said the thought of handling all those teats made him feel a bit peculiar.

'We must save our disappearing hedgerows at all costs,' Mum had said after her encounter with the JCB. She had dusted the pig-pooh off her maternity combat gear. (She'd gone to the Army Reject shop and managed to find a size 56 jacket. Amy had been really jealous.)

'Think of all the grub you can stuff in those pockets,' she'd said. 'My dad's got access this weekend. I'm going to make him get me one.'

As it turned out, Amy's dad bought himself one too. I saw them in the shopping mall. It looked really stupid with his cowboy hat and flared jeans.

The shack was looking quite decent now. An army of women had stomped through the mud one weekend to help get things straight. Fiona's laughing hyena had almost been shot for sheep-worrying but had thought it all a huge joke. Al had stood on the stairs directing operations. At least now the Kellogg's Cornflake and McVitie's Hob Nob cardboard boxes Al had demanded from the supermarket had been unpacked. She'd refused the boxes with Kerrygold Butter on the side saying it wasn't polyunsaturated.

A whole nest of spiders fell out of Al's Tina Turner wig when I unpacked it but Jed said we could always use it as a rug to go in front of the fire if she didn't fancy wearing it any more.

Jed had cooked everyone one of his delicious organic bean casseroles and we'd all sat round the paraffin stove coughing and enjoying the meal. Mum and her friends re-lived past battles. Jed was upstairs seeing to Rosa's kids. I didn't think they'd all fit on that straw mattress Al had made from a couple of old sacks. One complained it was a bit itchy but Rosa's gentle smack in the mouth had soon shut him up. I didn't like to tell him he had '25 Kilos Best British Potatoes' imprinted on the back of his pyjamas. He might have cried even louder.

I just sat there dreaming of Gazza. I'd invited him over but he said he was going Christmas shopping. I wondered if he was getting my present. An engagement ring, perhaps? Some theatrical make-up so I could practise being a star? Or maybe even a pair of gorgeous spotty shoes. If he did get them at least they'd match my ungorgeous spotty nose. He'd said only the week before my Reeboks looked stupid with my Crimplene pinafore dress. That was just one of the things I adored about Gazza — he always said the right thing at the right time.

I'd rescued Blossom's parcel from the bin. There were four grubby little baby suits. One still had Petal's dirty nappy in it but I threw it on the fire. I knew Mum would be annoyed because it was a disposable one. There were six little woolly cardigans. I didn't think our sweet baby would mind the smell. After all, stale sick would be just *one* of the aromas it would have to get used to. If the farmer hadn't decided to build a dung heap behind our hedge, it wouldn't have been so bad. Still, Jed looked really dishy with that peg on his nose. He'd had a job to get a real gold one but had eventually found one in Harrods.

There were also a couple of tiny sweet pink bonnets with bunnies on. I managed to dye them black and make the bunnies look like motor bikes with a green marker pen.

I heard Al talking on the phone.

'I've just been on to my Friend of the Earth,' she said. 'She's trying to make this area an SSSI.'

Jed smiled. 'What's that, darling? Sadistic . . . ? sexy . . . ?'

Al threw back her head and laughed. She did that a lot lately, especially when the baby kicked. Sometimes she

62

let me hold my hand over her bump when it did that. I managed to hide the bruises under my little red knitted mittens Blossom sent me. I was really pleased she'd chosen red. They matched my chilblains.

'No, gorgeous hunk.' Al gathered Jed to her swelling breast. 'Site of Special Scientific Interest.'

'Oh.' Jed breathed heavily into her boobs. A red flush of impending fatherhood came to his cheeks. 'Yes, it certainly is.'

'If it is made an SSSI then that wretched male farmer won't be able to grub out hedges, fill in ponds, and leave his dung just anywhere,' she said. 'Let alone pen all those poor chickens up in misery and inject his cows with all sorts of growth hormones.'

'I think he's rather dishy,' I said.

'You would, Charlie. If you had any taste at all you wouldn't go to see your father so often.'

'Oh, I don't know,' I said. 'Blossom's cooking's quite good.' I didn't tell her once Blossom had used wallpaper paste instead of tapioca. My real dad hadn't said anything. I think his lips must have been stuck together so he couldn't.

'That drudge,' Mum said scathingly. 'She's a disgrace to her sex. It's about time you persuaded her to come to my classes, Charlie.'

'Oh no,' Jed piped up. 'She's not pregnant *again*!'

'No, beloved . . . my Assertiveness Class. And I meant taste in *men*, Charlie. The fact that Blossom can cook is no recommendation at all. A woman needs to be assertive, not a damn kitchen worker, if she is to fulfil her potential.'

'And men,' Jed remarked timidly.

Al smiled and patted him on the pony tail. 'Yes, sweetie, but they've had a couple of million years' practice.'

'What about Gazza?' I said. 'He's quite assertive.' I thought of the time he asserted himself in the junior playground and got punched on the nose. He was only asking for his ball back.

Al frowned and breathed in deeply. She put her hand in the small of her back and winced.

'Now, don't push . . .' Jed said in a panic . . . 'just pant, let your breath out in short pants.'

'Short pants?' Al said. 'He doesn't still wear those, does he?'

'Who?' I shook my head and sighed. The people in my Mills and Boon books never talked to each other like this.

'Gazza,' my mum thundered. 'He doesn't wear short trousers does . . . ?'

'No, sweetness,' Jed said from the floor where he'd hurriedly gone to practise his exercises. He was lying with his hands together over his stomach. 'I'm trying to teach you to breathe properly.'

As usual, our conversation was getting us nowhere.

I went to my room to finish learning my lines. Even as an understudy I'd got to be word perfect. The newspaper I'd stuffed into the cracks in the walls was damp with rain. I moved the bin-bag out of the way and looked out of my window. The dung heap looked quite picturesque in the gloom of the winter twilight. The steam rising from it made a kind of aromatic haze over the landscape.

A cow mooed mournfully as it mourned its dear little calf gone to market only that day, and the sheep bleated in panic as they tried desperately to get away from the marauding gang of village dogs that patrolled the area. I heard the rustic, echoing bang, bang of the farmer's gun as he shot a rabbit or two and an agonized squawk from the chicken shed where one tried to peck its cell-mate's head off in a desperate attempt to find room to move around.

I wondered what Gazza was doing. Was he leaning from his window, looking out over the picturesque rooftops that stretched as far as the eye could see? Was he thinking of me? Was he plucking up the courage to lay his angel lips on mine?

If he didn't do it soon I thought I'd have a nervous breakdown.

Gazza had only visited our new shack once. His football had got bunged up with mud and he never came again. I'd brought him up to my room but none of the Seven Tips for a Sexy Snog had worked. Jed hadn't been to Tesco's so there hadn't been any grub to cook. Al had chucked all the wine over the jungle one night in a fit of remorse. She said why should we have such luxuries when so many species of wildlife were endangered. I didn't like to say she had probably killed a few million worms when she threw the wine away, or at least made them drunk and diswriggly. She was still mad because she'd been refused membership of Elefriends on account of her Access card being out of date. And when she tried to join the Mrs Tiggywinkle club they were very prickly about having an assertive member.

The soft light had turned to complete darkness when my torch batteries had run out and my efforts to sing along to ACDC on Al's portable karaoke machine had gone flat. My perfume bottle had gone a bit mouldy with damp and my sweet whispered promises fell on deaf ears. It could have been because it was so cold that Gazza had his Manchester United scarf wrapped round his ears and couldn't hear a word I was saying.

Anyway, he had to get home because the Big Match was on telly. He said Sharon Smith's dad had invited him to watch it at her house. I thought it was funny because Amy said they'd gone away on holiday and Sharon and her sister were on their own. Amy always got her facts wrong. She even thought low fat spread meant you had to sit on the floor to make your sandwiches.

*   *   *

I pinned the bin-bag back and sat on my bed reading the panto script. It was really hard to turn the pages with my mittens on. Downstairs I could hear Jed on his portable making the final arrangements for the Old Folk to come to the panto.

'Yes, yes,' he was saying. 'The mini-bus will be there at seven o'clock.'

The old person on the other end must have said something funny because Jed laughed. 'Don't worry,' he said. 'I'm sure two days will be long enough for them all to get over their trip to Euro-Disney — even if they had free drinks all the way there and back.'

On Friday, the dress rehearsal went true to form. I think it was mainly because Sonia Scissorhands broke a finger-nail trying to do up the clips that held Amy's costume together. I knew that canvas tent material would be difficult to fix. If Amy hadn't eaten fourteen hamburgers for supper it might have been different. After Sonia fainted with shock and Paddy tried to give her the kiss of life things settled down a bit. Mind you, I thought Paddy's ear would *never* stop bleeding where Sonia had almost sliced it off.

Sammy did his wheelchair wizard bit as usual and *almost* knocked Amy down when he made his entrance, stage left.

'Your Evil Step-Dad has ordered me to run you over,' he said, just managing to stop his chair falling from the stage as it bounced off Amy. He looked really hand-some in his woodman's costume. There was something about the old leather jacket of Al's that Sonia had accidentally cut all the way down the front that was *really* sexy. Or it could have been the axe my mum had tucked affectionately down by his side to make him look authentic.

Mum sat in the front row shouting instructions.

'Amy, for goodness' sake get up off the stage! We want no over-acting if you don't mind.'

'I'm trying,' Amy said breathlessly. She tried to retrieve the seven Bounty bars that had fallen out of the pockets of her gathered, medieval tent. I really didn't know why Sonia had made Amy wear that yellow blouse, it looked perfectly dreadful with that long black Cher wig and eight chins.

'What's your next line . . . ?' Al consulted her script. 'Oh yes . . . "You just try it and I'll punch your head in" . . . Come on, Amy!'

I could hear Sonia muttering something in the wings. It sounded like 'Friends, Romans, countrymen, lend me your ears,' but it couldn't have been that. For one thing, it was a new fingernail someone needed to lend her, not their ears. I couldn't actually see anything wrong with Sonia's ears although I must admit it was hard to see them under that Cleopatra hair piece. We were doing several performances, one to the school, one to the public, and one to the Old Folk and local VIPs. None of them were Romans, I felt sure. I suppose some of them *might* live in the country but they weren't exactly our friends.

To be honest, we weren't too popular at the moment. What with Al revving up the Kawasaki at all hours of the night and Jed playing his tapes *really* loud, I think people in the village wished we'd stayed away. Especially since Mum had liberated all the battery hens from their living hell and they were scratching up people's gardens in a desperate attempt to find their first ever worm. Although I think some of the country folk even preferred them to the newly-released, intensively-reared pigs whose delighted grunts and squeals drowned out the sound of their tellys.

With great difficulty my mum heaved herself out of the seat. After Jed had managed to prise off the chair stuck to her backside she approached the footlights. I was sitting in the wings with my arms round Gazza. He looked gorgeous in his Prince's costume. White tights, little (fake) fur jacket, silver lamé blouse and a crown made from a Kellogg's cornflake packet with gold foil on. Amy had been saving the foil from her Caramac bars. It had taken her at least ten minutes to get enough to cover the crown. Jed had made it with his artistic staple-gun and it fitted Gazza's head like a glove. I gently took his football away.

'Gazza, sweetheart, I'll look after that. You might be king of the first eleven but Snow White's Prince is having a picnic not a cup final.'

Sharon Smith came up to us wearing her Evil Step-Dad's costume. I think Sonia must have hooked it out at the Council's re-cycling centre. There's a big skip there you can put your old clothes in. When she first brought it to rehearsal I'd thought it might be my understudy's costume, but the cream flared jeans, flower-power shirt and Evil Step-Dad's tweed flat cap would never have suited me. My hair is much too thick to go under a flat-cap even though I rinse it in Sooper-shiny cream mousse. It didn't suit Sharon Smith much either. And I did wish she'd sewn some buttons on the shirt. No Evil Step-Dad ever had boobs like that.

I could hear singing from the dressing rooms. I supposed Mr Donovan was taking his job seriously and providing liquid refreshment for everyone. Or it could have been Ms Keegan putting on her Tone-up Hip and Thigh tape so the cast could get in shape.

I was just going to try to distract Gazza's fascinated stare from Sharon's missing buttons and whispering 'wicked' under his breath, when I heard a commotion from the front of the house.

When I peeped round the curtains I saw Jed slumped in a chair holding his stomach. His pony tail had come out of its little ribbon and his Artistic Creator's cream and turquoise loose-fitting shirt was all creased.

'It's all right, sweetie,' Al was saying. 'It's a false alarm.' She motioned to a couple of her body-building friends.

'Take him home,' she commanded. 'I'm afraid he's getting near his time.'

On his way out Jed managed to gasp over the Body Builder's massive shoulder. 'Let Charlie take your part, sweetie. We can't have a policeman giving birth on stage. After all, Snow White's supposed to be the star.'

Al patted his forehead. 'All right, hunks, whatever you say.'

After I'd picked myself up from the floor with shock at hearing her say that, I heard Mum call me down. I was so excited my knees were trembling. This could be my big break . . . the moment I'd been waiting for ever since I'd decided to become an actor. It seemed a lifetime although it must have been all of three months. I'd got holes in both my tights so you could actually hear my knees banging together like maracas. In fact, Wanda took her headphones off for a second and said:

'Hey, man, spot that tune!'

'Beethoven's Fifth,' Mick-the-Dick said.

'Don't be stoopid!' Paddy got hold of Mick's jumper. 'It ain't nuffin of the sort.'

'Yes, it is!' Sammy pushed Paddy in the back of the knees with one of his wheels. 'So just watch it, Paddy.'

Paddy growled something tough and picked furiously at the spot on his chin. His pink and gold-winged Dear Mother spectacles fell in his glass of lager. He fished them out, still swearing, and wiped them on his royal silver and diamond encrusted frock.

'Mum,' I said, breathlessly, expecting any minute to be an overnight success. 'Are you sure Jed's all right?'

'Yes, Charlie, just a false labour pain. Nothing to worry about. He's well prepared.'

'No, Mum . . . not that.' I was still in shock. 'You didn't assert yourself.'

'What?' She frowned, the tattoo on her forehead changing shape as it always did when she was puzzled.

'With Jed . . .' I spluttered. 'You said "whatever you say".'

She smiled. 'Charlie, we have to be careful with these pregnant fathers. Handle them with kid gloves. Well . . .' she waved her studded gauntlets in the air. 'Not quite *kid* gloves in my case. It's a very emotional time in their life, you know.'

'Yes,' I agreed. 'He cries more at ante-natal clinic than any of the others.'

She didn't say any more about me playing the Police-person so I guessed she'd just agreed with Jed because he was having an emotional moment.

She shook her head. 'I have told him to be brave, it's a perfectly natural thing — ' she broke off.

Outside, a couple of DIPPOS had managed to escape the clutches of the Body Bs and were banging on the window. We turned to see a banner soar into the air and a mass of arms and legs where someone had done a flying rugby-tackle. Mum tutted in consternation.

'I hope she's all right.'

'I think it's just the banner that's broken.'

Al looked at me in disgust. 'No, Charlie. Who the hell cares about the DIPPOS? I was concerned for my mate. She's got a Ms Gladiator contest next week and doesn't want any scars.'

On stage, Amy was forgetting her lines.The Six Small Persons were really too big to get on the stage with her all at once, so one or two stayed in the wings. I could hear Wanda's feet drumming as she did the Lambada with a chair and the clatter of Jason's bottle against his glass.

'I'll work down the mine,' Amy's prompt was saying, 'and you stay here and do the household routine.'

'Very well,' Ms Keegan as a Small Person shouted through her false beard. 'To a count of four . . . one, two, three, four . . . OK, eight lunges, four half-stars and *march* . . . step it out now, knees high . . .!'

'No, Ms Keegan,' Mum shouted assertively. 'You're supposed to say . . . "Anything you say, Snow White, baby".'

'Oh, sorry . . .' Ms Keegan hitched up her leotard. I didn't know why she had to wear her cycling helmet, I've never seen one in a pantomime before.

The rest of the dress rehearsal went OK. There was one incident when a DIPPO managed to escape the clutches of the vigilantes and infiltrate the hall.

The first we knew of it was when a chair came hurtling on to the stage and knocked Gazza's crown off.

Al turned in anger.

'Out!' she yelled, struggling to maintain her equilibrium. Not easy when you've got a bump the size of a shack. 'Get that DIPPO out.'

Sonia teetered up the aisle on her delicious spotty high heels waving her hands. The DIPPO scarpered in panic, trying to clutch his torn anorak around him. I didn't know how he'd manage to explain those scratches on his back to his wife.

After that the show proceeded as normal. We managed to wake Paddy up in time to do his lines and Amy only left the stage four times to have a snack. Admittedly, we all got a bit hoarse trying to make Wanda hear what was going on but a couple of squirts from Sonia's antiseptic theatrical throat spray helped no end. We persuaded Mary to leave her post in front of the mirror for five minutes to say her lines and Mr Donovan looked brilliant in his Father Christmas outfit, even if his hands did shake a bit. He really looked the part although he did keep getting his heel caught in his tunic when he was reeling about on his knees. Sonia promised to take the hem up for him but he said he felt shure Missish Wally

71

would do it when she finished polishing the brassh in the Shmall Pershons' cottage.

We all applauded when he got his lines right after thirty-five takes.

' . . .Will we be allowed to go to the Prinsh and Coffin for a couple of jars at lunchtime, Shnow White, Shir . . .' Jason managed before finally sinking back into the twilight zone to be heard from no more.

There was still no sign of Al's mystery star guest playing the part of the seventh Small Person but she assured us she still had a surprise up her sleeve.

That was the moment when Paddy yelled — 'And what's that up your jumper, missis? Scotch mist?'

Al had already thrown her bum bag at him so she resorted to being assertive this time. Poor Paddy's nose would never look the same with the ring torn out.

'If only he wouldn't call me Mrs,' Mum remarked, dusting down her smock.

Before the final curtain she said to me, 'Charlie . . . I think you'll have to take over my part as Policeperson, after all.' She put her hand on her bump and smiled maternally.

'Why?' I said, my heart drumming with excitement. I clutched her, feeling the hard muscles of her forearm. 'Is the baby . . . ?'

She grinned, her bright green and lemon striped eyeshadow and midnight-blue false eyelashes gave her a kind of maternal show-biz glow. 'Not quite yet, Charlie, but I promised Jed I'd give up the part. You know a man isn't worth his salt who doesn't keep his promises.'

'Salt?' Amy said, wriggling inside her tent. 'Not with ice-cream, thank you.'

8

I was really excited about getting the part of the Police-person. I had this feeling it would be my big chance. I knew I wouldn't exactly win an Oscar for my performance but a standing ovation would be almost as good.

Even Horoscope Horace, my star-teller, said I would be getting a lot of surprises that week. Maybe being an overnight success would be one of them. I still hoped my first kiss would be another. I was dying of love for Gazza and all he did was peer at me through his rose-coloured specs and say stuff like . . .

'Good job you didn't dress up, Charlie.'

Gazza's idea of dressing up was wearing a shell tracksuit with 'Soccer is Brill' embroidered on the back. I hate to be disloyal but Gazza really hasn't got a lot of dress sense lately. He used to have a really fab green satin jacket but threw it away when someone said he looked like an unripe tomato. I'd even tried to seduce him by wearing my LA Raider's gear off-the-shoulder but he'd only used the shoulder-pads to practise dribbling with.

I was so desperate to feel his honey lips on mine I even asked Al what I could do about my spot. I didn't think Gazza would ever kiss me until it disappeared.

'It's just your hormones, Charlie,' she said, looking up

from her *Mother-to-Be Motorbike Maniac* mag. 'Spots are part of growing up.'

'Well, if having Mount Everest on the end of your nose is growing up, then you can keep it.'

I knew that rule number one for Seven Tips for a Sexy Snog had got to be a spotless nose, even though the Teenage Sexpert who'd written down the tips didn't say anything about it. I suppose he thought it must be obvious to anyone with brains. And you certainly didn't get thickos reading that kind of mag.

My mum laughed and shoved one of our free-range hens down off the table. It wasn't actually *our* hen. It had taken refuge in our shack after Al let it out. I don't think it appreciated being chased by a marauding fox although Al said it was better to die naturally in the jaws of a wild animal than be bludgeoned to death by a cell-mate who'd had its beak removed to stop it pecking. 'Never mind, Charlie,' she said when I looked miserably down at my spot, 'you'll soon be a woman, independent and equal.'

'I'll never be a woman until Gazza kisses me,' I moaned, picking the egg up and putting it in the larder.

'Surely you're not waiting for him to make the first move?' Al said in horror. 'Honestly, Charlie, you are a twit. I've told you, if you want it, go for it.' She sighed and patted her mountainous stomach. 'Have all my lectures been for nothing?'

'I thought you charged for them,' I said, remembering one of her posters Jed had creatively created. I had seen it at a meeting at the Council for the Protection of Rural England headquarters. I felt sure it said five quid an hour.

'No, Charlie . . . my lectures to you. Everything I've taught you about equality and assertiveness and cleaning out the carburettor on a Harley Davidson.'

'Oh, those,' I sighed. 'I thought you meant something important.'

Just then Jed came in from his Creative Consultancy with a headache.

'I must be coming out in sympathy,' he said, brushing a well-manicured hand across his brow as Al led him up the ladder to their bedroom to practise her aroma-therapy.

'Well, *I'm* coming out in spots,' I said, going back to Jed's *New Man Health and Handsomeness* mag. Maybe I'd find the answer in there?

As it was, all I found were earwigs.

Later, when they came down smelling of extract of deadly nightshade and cinnamon, Mum said the outfit she wore to the Mayor's civic reception would do as a Policeperson's costume if I really insisted on having one. Without the diamanté and jet drop ear-rings, of course.

'Not likely,' I said. 'I'll look a right twit in a chef's jacket dyed dark blue, combat trousers and a Postman Pat cap. Even if Jed has sewn shiny buttons on.'

'Charlie, are you being assertive?' Mum asked me delightedly.

'Yes.' I took the rollers out of my hair. The mouse's nest in one of them almost fell out. 'I'm getting a proper uniform so you can take a running jump.'

'Not in our condition, we can't,' Jed said. He looked up from his *Mother and Baby* mag. 'It says here, any exercise whilst pregnant should be gentle and controlled.'

'Yes,' Al looked at him lovingly. 'You always are, Jed.'

'Well,' I said, peering into the broken bit of glass that served as a mirror. 'When are we going to get it? Time's running out, you know.'

I shook my head so a whirl of soft curls fell around my face. The candlelight reflected highlights in my hair *and* the highlights in the spot on my nose. I would just die if it didn't go away before our first performance. I mean, whoever saw a copper with a zit? Bruises, yes . . . a black eye . . . quite often, but a zit . . . never! I mean, who in *The Bill*'s got acne?

I'd already tried lots of things to get rid of it. Jed had even made me a mud pack from the front garden but it hadn't done any good. All I got was a drunken worm crawling up my nostril. I could see I'd have to resort to wearing Al's Captain Pugwash look-alike mask although I felt sure he hadn't been a captain in the police force. And I knew Gazza would *never* fancy me sexually whilst I had that on. He'd certainly never kissed Sharon Smith and she looked like Captain Pugwash without a mask on.

'I told you, Charlie,' Al said. 'It's not due quite yet.'

'No, Mum, the panto . . . it's on next week and I haven't got anything to wear yet.'

Jed sighed and rubbed a swollen ankle. 'I'll take you to the Remand Centre on the way to my class. I hear they've got a whole load of police uniforms some of the inmates were dressed in when they were copped.'

'Great!' I used my hairbrush to brush up the fluff on my sweet white bolero Mary Hadda gave me. It had lipstick stains on the front but they hardly showed. 'When? It's the opening night on Thursday — a star must be ready for her first performance.'

'Don't let this go to your head, Charlie,' Mum waved her helmet at me.

'Oh, Mum.' I hugged her bump. 'You know it's miles too big.'

On the way to the Remand Centre we stopped off at my real dad's to deliver their panto tickets.

'I think I'd better stay outside,' Jed said, thumbing through his *Guide to Painless Childbirth*. 'I'll just memorize another chapter while you're in there. It's my last class tonight.'

I hugged Blossom and Timmie. Petal was asleep in the coal shed in her pram.

'It's the only place where you can't hear the crowds chanting,' Blossom explained.

76

I shouted 'hello' to my real dad. He waved his cigarette at me. 'Score's fifteen nil, Charlie,' he said.

'Great!'

My real dad turned in a haze of fag smoke. 'It's not great at all, Charlie,' he said. 'It *could* have been twenty-five nil if they'd put the boot in a bit more.'

'In where?' I said, puzzled.

'In the other players' faces, Charlie.' My real dad looked at me as if I was daft. 'It's obvious you don't know anything about the rules of football.'

'Yes, she does,' Blossom said. Her little work-worn hand with its dear jagged fingernails flew to her mouth when she realized she had disagreed with him. But my real dad hardly noticed.

'No, she doesn't,' he mumbled. 'Make a cup of tea.'

'There isn't any tea,' Blossom blurted bravely.

'Yes, there is. I saw a couple of tea bags under the wheel of Timmie's Mad Max Action motor bike.'

I followed Blossom's tired footsteps into the kitchen. Timmie was under the table playing *The Evil Dead* with a carving knife. I just managed to rescue the cat although it looked a bit bald round the throat.

'I've brought your panto tickets,' I said, taking them out of my little lurex handbag.

Blossom wiped her brow. 'Ooh, lovely, thank you, Charlie.' She began putting the ingredients into a bowl to make a cake. 'Are you in it?'

I told her of my various roles. Understudy to Snow White, person in charge of publicity, and Policeperson.

'Do you have to say much?' Blossom popped the cake into the oven, made the tea, cut some bread, wiped the Kattomeat from around Timmie's sweet, rosebud mouth, washed her thumb under the tap where he bit it, rinsed a couple of my real dad's shirts in environmentally un-friendly washing powder and put three teaspoons of sugar in her tea. 'I need it to give me energy,' she explained.

'No you don't.' My real dad stood propping up the doorway. 'Where's that blasted tea? A working man could die of thirst waiting to be waited on.'

'I've got some very important lines,' I explained when Blossom came back from taking in my real dad's mug of tea. 'After all, as Mum says, you can't have an Evil Step-Dad trying to bump off someone without getting arrested.'

'Yes, you can,' my real dad yelled from the front room. 'What about Jack the Ripper?'

'Was he a step-dad?' I shouted back.

'Well, he took steps down dark alleys, didn't he?'

'Ignore him,' Blossom said rebelliously.

I looked at her suspiciously. 'Blossom, have you been going to assertiveness classes?'

'No,' she whispered. 'But I found this book up in the attic. I think it must have belonged to your mum.' She reached into the pocket of her dear little stained pinny.

How To Reach Your Potential As a Woman in Two Thousand Easy Lessons, it said. (The book not the pinny. The pinny had a poem on the front):

What is a Wife?

A wife will cuddle you
And wash away your blues
She'll love you for ever
And polish your shoes
She'll rub and she'll scrub
Her work's never done
And when she dies of exhaustion
We'll find you another one.

Under that was an advertisement for the Find-a-Mug Computer Dating Agency. I guessed my dad had got the pinny as a free gift before he met Blossom.

I looked at the book Blossom had placed secretively in my hand.

78

'I bet Dad didn't know it was there,' I giggled, helping myself to a slice of cake. It was a bit soggy. I think Timmie must have chewed it before me.

Blossom put a chapped finger over her lips. 'I found it three weeks ago. I've had time to read half a page already.'

At that rate, I thought, it'd be a hundred years before Blossom 'saw the light' as Al put it. Mind you, everything was OK at my real dad's now Blossom had fixed the fuse. And why she couldn't just be content to be a wife and mother, I didn't know. She seemed to have so much I desperately yearned for. A house, children, ironing, washing, cooking, running little errands . . . a nose without a spot on the end.

'Blossom!' my real dad called from in front of the telly. 'Another cup!'

Blossom made a face at me and trotted slowly off to obey his command.

I followed her into the front room. 'I've brought your panto tickets, Dad.'

He waved his hand. 'Great, Charlie. Put them on the sideboard, I'll look at them when the match's finished.'

On the telly, there were so many players felled by the Isle of Wight Killers it looked like the invasion of the body snatchers.

I knelt by my real dad's chair. 'You will come, won't you, Dad? It's going to be great.'

'No, it's not,' he said. 'But I'll come anyway. *She's* not in it, is she? Not playing the giant?'

'There's no giant in *Snow White*, Dad,' I said lovingly.

'There would be if she was in it,' he retorted, blowing smoke affectionately into my face. 'A giant pain in the neck.'

I heard Blossom giggle from the doorway. I thought at first someone had said something funny but she was only laughing at Timmie as he ripped up the *Satellite Times*.

I knew Jed would have memorized his chapter of G.P.C. by now so I said I'd got to go.

'See you Saturday, Dad.'

'No, you won't,' he said. 'But we'll see you if you're the star, won't we, Blossom?'

'She's not exactly the star,' Blossom said.

The last thing I saw was my dad almost fainting with horror. I thought at first the Isle of Wight had scored again but they hadn't. He almost passed out because not only had Blossom made a feeble attempt at being assertive, Timmie had eaten all his cigarette papers while he wasn't looking!

There was no one about at the High Security Remand Centre so we just went in and helped ourselves to a Policeperson's outfit. It didn't take long to find one that fitted me. I left my jeans and baseball cap as security. I didn't think anyone would fancy a second-hand Laura Ashley one hundred per cent pure cotton blouse with the frills cut off so I kept that on. Jed left a note just in case anyone noticed the uniform had gone. He promised to return it after the final performance.

We arrived at the Ante-Natal clinic just in time for the relaxation class.

A few mums waddled towards us. 'Jed . . . darling!' They marched him off to have a drink of vitamin-enriched milk before the class began.

There were lots of posters on the wall. 'How to Practise Safe Sex' with the slogan 'Carry a Condom in your Handbag'. I made a mental note to tell Jed. Then there was one giving a list of sexually transmitted diseases and the dangers of alcohol and drug abuse. Their bright colours and funny little cartoon illustrations really cheered the place up. Especially one of a kid lying in a coffin surrounded by empty ozone-unfriendly aerosol cans of solvent.

There weren't any posters about being assertive, doing tap dancing classes or the next gig starring Deathshead Condom so I guessed Al hadn't had time to do her rounds. Mind you, she had taken maternity leave from her job on the building site so it was only a matter of time. I'd seen a poster advertising her Childbirth For Men lecture in the lobby of the Remand Centre so I knew she'd been there.

In the other room I could hear Jed chatting with the other mums and dads and showing them the little cot-blanket he'd crocheted.

'I feel like a new man,' he was saying. 'I can recommend crocheting to you all.'

There was a chorus of maternal giggles and then noises like the rushing of wind in the trees as they all practised their breathing exercises. Then I heard clapping and stamping of feet. I thought Jed was doing his Mick Jagger impersonation but when I went in, two mums with one of the dads squashed between them had managed to crowd around Jed. They were fanning him with their Mothercare catalogues.

'What's up, Jed?' I called. 'You having contractions?'

The mums looked at me over their stomachs.

'Have you come with a patrol car to escort him to hospital?'

I looked down at my costume. 'No — we're having the baby at home. I'm starring in the panto as a Policeperson actually.'

'You're right,' some pregnant person said. 'This whole thing's a bloody pantomime if you ask me.'

'Just because it's your tenth, Mrs Hubbard,' another bow-fronted lady said. 'We really thought you'd have mastered the exercises by now.'

'... Or the art of family planning,' someone snickered.

The walls of the clinic rumbled with expectant laughter.

'We were just applauding Jed's bravery,' they said, 'and he came over a bit strange.'

81

'Bravery?'

'Yes . . . it hasn't been an easy pregnancy — what with moving house, artistically directing the panto, and now he's produced this wonderful little fluffy blanket . . .'

'Oh . . .?' I said.

Jed was looking a bit pale and his Yves St Laurent cardi was all creased where he'd been sitting with his head between his knees.

All of a sudden there was a bang and a crash as someone swept through the door. She clapped her hands together.

'OK, you crummy lot . . . on the floor with your hands over your heads!'

I thought at first a bank robber had mistaken the clinic for Barclays but I soon realized it was the maternity nurse. And what's more . . . I recognized her. She had been one of Al's assertive mates who'd camped with us on our demo to save Toadstool Wood. She was a FFART (Females Fight Against the Rape of Toadstool Wood).

'Oh dear . . .' wailed Jed suddenly, 'I've forgotten my cushion.'

The nurse frowned. 'Stupid twit . . . honestly, you blokes know nothing about having babies!' She wrenched a cupboard door open. 'Here . . .!'

I caught the cushion and helped Jed sit down with his back propped up against the wall. I think the cushion must have been used at the Baby Clinic because there was something nasty sticking to it but Jed didn't seem to notice.

The nurse stared at me. 'Didn't know you'd joined the fuzz, Charlie.'

Before I had time to answer she opened her bag and laid a row of shiny instruments on the table.

'I'll demonstrate these later,' Nurse F. said with an evil grin.

Jed went pale. 'Charlie,' he hissed, 'I feel sick.'

'Oh, Jed, I thought that was only for the first three months.'

82

I didn't say any more. The gorgon look the nurse threw me reminded me of that caretaker in *Grange Hill* when the kids pinch stuff out of his cupboard. Although when she'd opened hers I could see it was full of baby food and bottles of gin so it was obvious it hadn't been raided.

'OK . . . !' She clapped her hands as the other mums scurried to sit down. One or two mistakenly pulled their partners down too and for a minute the floor looked like the aftermath of the battle of the bulge. 'Come on, you lot,' Nurse F. yelled. 'Relax!'

I sat beside Jed and helped him do his exercises. He had trouble starting. Instead of relaxing his toes up through his calves, knees, thighs, tummy, etc., I think he must have done it the wrong way round. Certainly when all the others were shrugging their shoulders back he was sitting with his legs outstretched and his feet in the air.

Nurse F. went to the tape machine and put on the music. I really didn't think 'Great Balls of Fire' was totally suited to the occasion but nobody dared complain.

'Right . . . !' Nurse shouted above Jerry Lee. 'You'd all better be lying comfortably or else . . .' I helped Jed wedge the cushion underneath his bent knees. 'As you're all near your time,' she went on, '. . . we're going to practise our three stages of breathing right up to our delivery technique.'

I wasn't quite sure what the post office had to do with it but didn't dare ask. After all, if I was to be a wife and mother one day I'd need to know all kinds of techniques.

By the time we got to the delivery stage, Jed was exhausted.

'I don't know about relaxation classes,' he whispered through his cushion, 'I'm knackered.'

'No talking, Jed!' Nurse F. shouted. She peered at me over the top of her glasses. 'You're not taking him into

83

custody, are you? Prison's no place for new-born babies, you know.'

I grinned. 'No, I'm trying to eliminate him from my enquiries.'

Nurse F. frowned. 'Well, if he's guilty, I hope he doesn't get sentenced to hard labour.'

The mums rolled around, laughing.

'For God's sake, you lot,' Nurse F. bellowed, 'you're not supposed to be *enjoying* this!' She came to bend down beside Jed. She patted his brow, then wiped the sweat off her fingers on her skirt. 'Are you quite sure you know what to do, Jed? You won't push when you should pant, or pant when you should push, now, will you?'

Jed looked confused. 'I . . . I hope not,' he stuttered.

'If you do,' she went on, 'labour could last for hours and hours and you could end up in stitches.'

I didn't honestly think it was that funny.

'Don't worry,' I said to Nurse F. as the other mums burped amongst themselves. 'My mum's got everything under control.'

Jed giggled as the nurse helped him to his feet. The others rolled over on to all fours and crawled around like camels with their humps upside down until their partners hauled them upright.

'You'd better take him home, Officer,' Nurse F. said. 'The excitement's a bit much for him. He's in such a state, I don't know how he's going to hold the video camera steady while Ms Scroggins has his baby.'

I took Jed's arm. 'He'll manage,' I said. 'Or else he'll be in the dog house.'

'Not getting a dog too, are you?' another round lady called as she staggered to her feet. 'I would have thought two kids and Jed were enough for anybody.'

I grinned and managed to squeeze past her through the door. 'No, but Mum's thinking about calling the baby Lassie.'

'What happens if it's a boy?'

'That's if it *is* a boy,' I called as we staggered out. 'If it's a girl she's probably calling it Elvis.'

Jed dropped me off at the shopping mall. I was still on the lookout for a gorgeous pair of polka-dot shoes. I thought I could wear them to the after-performance celebration party. They'd look great with my black leggings, cut-off-short denim hot-pants and pink Lycra boob-tubes Amy had given me. There had actually only been one boob-tube but Jed had cut it up and made six. Amy's mum had got it out of the catalogue but it had never fitted her properly. They only went up to a size extra-extra-extra. Jed said he'd never pay six ninety-nine for a boob-tube but paying it for half a dozen wasn't bad. Trouble was, he'd only had green cotton but I could always wear emerald eye shadow to match the stitches.

I spotted Miss Lamb in the beauty salon getting an all-over massage and body tone. It looked like her sports car boyfriend in a white overall doing it but it must have been a beautician. Unless he'd got a new job. Last I heard he was running the Pensioners' Sweetheart Dating Agency.

I did a tour of the charity shops but there weren't any polka-dot shoes. There were a couple of pairs of brown sandals and a pair of baseball boots with holes in but I didn't fancy them. You've got to have just the right shoes to complete an outfit. It says it in all the mags. Well . . . not Jed's *Good Parenthood* — but most of the others. I did try the size 12 baseball boots on. I don't know why the old lady behind the counter giggled.

'They don't go with your helmet,' she smirked. 'What are you, constable or sergeant?'

I was going to say I could always stuff recycled kitchen roll in the toes of the boots but couldn't be bothered.

*   *   *

On the way to the bus-stop I passed the Old Folk's Day Centre. Their minibus was parked outside so they must have got back from Euro-Disney OK. The air-brushed picture of Hitler being blown to bits on the side looked really great. I wondered if Jed's Creative Consultancy had created it.

There were a few of the old folk inside the building. I could see them jigging around to Michael Jackson's Greatest Hits. The shouting and yelling must have been them singing along. I could see a couple snogging in the canteen. It must have been really hard for the man to kiss the lady while she was wearing that Euro-Disney Mademoiselle Minnie Mouse costume. It looked as if the nose kept getting in the way. Not that I would mind snogging with Gazza even if he was wearing the strip of the entire England team and a Monsieur Mickey Mouse mask as well.

I'd just bent down to pick up a couple of McDonald's environmentally-friendly discarded Big Mac and French fries boxes to put in the litter bin when someone hurtled down the steps in front of me. When I stood up, he looked at me in horror. I know my spot looked pretty mean but the rest of me wasn't that bad. I thought at first it might have been because I'd dyed my hair green to match the moss growing on the wall of our front room. Then, the bloke threw something at me and scarpered. His running vest had something printed on the back but I couldn't make out what. Maybe he was practising for the Olympics or something? He certainly shot round the corner faster than Michael J. Fox's car in *Back to the Future*. If it had been Michael J. Fox I'd have run after him.

I picked up the bunch of keys and the bag he'd chucked at me. Inside the Day Centre some old guy was sorting through a pile of *Playboy* magazines and old, well-thumbed copies of the *Sunday Sport*. He wiped the sweat off his forehead with a shaky hand and looked at me.

'Someone practising for the Pensioners' Olympics dropped these,' I said, chucking the keys and the bag on his table. 'You'd better give them to him when he gets back.'

'Thank you, Officer,' the old guy said, hurriedly stuffing the mags into his brown shopping bag.

I thought how great it was that everyone was joining in the spirit of the panto by pretending I was a real policeperson. By the look of three ladies asleep in the corner surrounded by empty bottles, they'd been joining in the spirit of something too. Especially the one with the Cinderella frock on.

Just then there was a shout from the kitchen and loads of old folk came haring out. One old lady was waving a pint mug at me and another looked as if she wanted to shove her Donald Duck lollypop right up my nose.

I remembered then that Paddy Powell had been chased from the Day Centre last week. He'd only gone in to ask some old lady where she'd got her tattoos done. Actually, he'd had a lucky escape. One of the whisky bottles they'd chucked at him missed his head by inches. I thought of what whisky would do to *my* hair and make-up and legged it quick. A whole horde of them ran up the road after me but I hid in the graveyard. I knew none of them would follow me in there. I knew old folk don't like tempting providence. I reckoned it was a good job I hadn't got Sonia's wonderful spotty shoes on. I'd never have been able to out-run them in those.

9

I've been trying to decide which of my dreams is the most important. They are:

1) To get rid of my zit by fair means or foul.
2) a) To get Gazza to kiss me   ditto   ditto.
   b) To get some spotty shoes by ditto ditto.
3) To be an actor   ditto   ditto.
4) To train as a secretary or midwife   ditto   ditto.
5) To be a wife and mother etc., etc.

I thought about writing to Billy Brokenheart again but decided against it. I'd gone off him since he told some guy with body odour to try rubbing half an onion under his arms. With half the world starving I thought it was dead wasteful. I didn't really think he'd know anything about spotty noses, or spotty shoes for that matter.

By the time we staged our first performance of the panto our shack looked like backstage at Pinewood Studios. Amy's costume took up the entire front room and the pile of Small Persons' clothes looked like a boot sale no one had come to. Luckily, Jed had persuaded Sonia Scissorhands to let him make them. I think it was

Ms Keegan who refused to wear shredded dungarees over her cycling shorts and pink leotard.

Jed had been painting the scenery in the kitchen and the place looked like Joseph's amazing Technicolor dreamcoat. Mind you, I much preferred the interior of the Evil Step-Dad's castle to crumbling wattle and daub.

Jed was in a state as usual. Al blamed it on their condition.

'I dunno, Charlie,' she said. 'If men had to have babies we wouldn't have to push so hard to get anything done.'

On the day we were doing the panto for the old folk Jed was late getting home from shopping. Al thought maybe he was trying to find an assistant in Texas Homecare but it turned out he'd been looking for a new brand of grease-remover he'd seen advertised in Al's *Biker Beautiful* magazine.

He came in, twisting his ear-ring like mad, his personal stereo tinkling hypnotically. Jed had given up Des O'Connor and the Gypsy Kings for one of those Relaxation for Mothers-to-Be tapes. Trouble was, he kept falling asleep.

To cap it all (or helmet in this case) Al was doing her nut because she couldn't get her Kawasaki back together properly.

'Don't worry, sweetness,' Jed yawned. He put his Top Man bags on the table and threaded his way through the engine parts to light the paraffin stove. 'There's nothing wrong with you driving the BMW for a while. It does use lead-free, you know.' He took off his designer waxed jacket and threw it on to a tea chest, kicked off his green wellies, and prised the slugs out of his socks with a sigh.

Mum dismissed his words with a toss of her crew cut. She took a swig of vitamin-supplemented mineral water and stormed out of the door. I thought at first it was an earth tremor but it was only Al waddling pregnantly through the jungle to the outside loo.

'There's a crowd of DIPPOS outside,' she announced calmly when she came back. 'Stupid twits.' She quickly donned her maternity combat jacket and elasticated combat trousers. She bent to lace her boots. When Jed and me had helped her stand up straight again she took her truncheon from the larder.

'What shall we do?' Jed wrung his hands into his apron.

Al patted his head maternally with her truncheon. 'Now, don't you worry, hunky. I've got them sussed. There's a band of CRAPPS waiting at the school gates.'

'CRAPPS?' I asked. 'Surely the panto's not *that* bad?'

'No, Charlie — Campaign Rally to Actively Prevent Pantomime Sexism. Get those costumes packed. By the time the DIPPOS get themselves out of the mud we'll be long gone.' She raised her fist in the air. 'United we stand,' she shouted.

'Oh, Mum,' I wailed, polishing my buttons furiously. 'Not football, please. I hear enough about it from my sweet angel. And what shall I do about my make-up?'

'With a zit like that there's nothing much you can do . . . here . . .' She tossed me her Captain Pugwash mask with a grin. 'Wear this.'

'Get lost,' I said.

We thundered out of the back door (well . . . it's actually a sack pinned across the doorway) and piled into the BMW. From the front we could hear the groans and grunts of the DIPPOS as they tried to get their Hunter boots out of the mud. Or it could have been Al's liberated intensively-reared pigs intensively biting their backsides.

I didn't realize until it was too late that I'd forgotten to change my shoes. I mean, whoever saw a policeperson

90

wearing fluffy honey-monster slippers? Even if they were slightly bald. Whoever had them before me must have spilt treacle or something on them then tried to comb it off. Anyway, yukky brown nylon shag-pile definitely doesn't go with navy blue — not by any stretch of the imagination.

It was really hard trying to hang on to the Evil Step-Dad's castle as we roared up the motorway. I was convinced Jed should have been driving. Although my mum's got quite long arms, sitting in the back seat because you can't get behind the steering wheel's pretty stupid if you ask me.

The policeman in the panda car that overtook us in the fast lane looked really surprised. I suppose seeing a BMW with a castle sticking out of the side window and no one driving must be a pretty rare sight. Anyway, he only had to look on the roof and he would have seen Jed clinging on to Amy's tent for dear life. I suppose he did look weird wearing several Small Persons' costumes and three false beards but after all, it was almost Christmas. And when I saluted the policeman from the passenger seat he seemed to think everything was OK. It was a good job there were no other cars about otherwise the shower of gravel that flew up when the panda car roared off doing a ton down the central reservation might have broken someone's windscreen.

At school, an army of CRAPPS stood guard at the gates. I recognized several Body Bs, a dozen or so battered wives, several women from Al's assertiveness class, and a couple of tap dancers. The assertiveness pupils must have been getting into practice because when the Headmaster tried to get through on his moped they asserted themselves. I saw one of them doing a body search on him but he was smiling so he couldn't have minded too much. I heard Fiona's hyena, Giggles,

91

cracking up so he must have thought the whole performance was pretty hilarious. In fact, there was a carnival atmosphere about the whole thing. Maybe it was Rosa's kids entertaining everyone with their synchronized limbo-dancing under the school railings that did it?

The cast formed a guard of honour outside the hall. The Mayor was there looking like the hunchback of Notre Dame. It really was about time they found a chain for him that wasn't quite so heavy. The party of old folk waved their Euro-Dis flags like mad when we piled out of the car. One of them ran up to Mum, curtsied and presented her with a video of *Cinderella* and a little wooden replica of the Wicked Stepmother. She chucked them back at him.

'Have you never heard of CRAPPS?' she thundered. 'Campaign Rally to Actively Prevent Pantomime Sexism?'

The old chap curtsied again. 'Prevent it?' he said, looking disappointed and wiping the blood from his head wound. 'But that's why we're all here?'

Al frowned, her tattoo doing its shape-shifting job as usual. 'I don't understand.'

'Someone said there was sex in it, that's what we came for. There's nothing like a bit of sex to liven the place up a bit.'

Several old ladies giggled and waved their Macho Model calendars. One lost her balance and almost broke her ankle in her zimmer frame.

Al shoved the old chap aside. 'Explain to him, Charlie,' she commanded.

'Not me,' I said. 'I've got to prepare myself for my starring role.'

We all went inside. Gradually the cheering died down and we guessed Mary Hadda was explaining all about sex to the old folk. Then another roar went up and we guessed the DIPPOS had turned up at last. Or maybe the

92

pensioners had got the hang of the sex lessons and were making up for lost time?

Gazza was already in the dressing rooms. Actually, it looked more like undressing rooms with Sharon Smith trying to decide whether her flower-power shirt looked better with or without the pretty fluffy bobbles Jed had sewn on instead of buttons. Gazza was trying to do one up.

'Yo, Officer,' Sharon piped up.

I knew she was only giggling because she was jealous not only of my starring role but of my star-struck relationship with Gaz. I ignored her. After all, a star must retain her dignity even in the face of an unbuttoned flower-power shirt.

The curtain rose to thunderous applause. I guessed it was because the Body Bs had asserted themselves outside, routed the DIPPOS, and were waving their muscles threateningly at the audience. Deathshead Condom played a few heavy metal bars of their hit single 'Shut Yer Face or I'll have Yer Guts' and all went quiet.

The performance had begun.

I knew when Amy fell off the stage that things weren't going quite right. Mind you, the eighteen old folk who helped her back on did a great job. I knew a couple of them were instructors at the Power Lifting for the Over Seventies club in town because I'd seen them practising with baked-bean cans in the supermarket.

Luckily Blossom had brought her little carpenter's outfit and she soon hammered the floorboards back together. I didn't think Deathshead Condom would ever be the same again. I knew they shouldn't have been headbanging right in front of the stage like that. One looked really nutty with a broken plank nailed to her bass guitar. I saw my mum giving Blossom a thunderous look but I don't think she realized quite who she was scowling at. For one thing Blossom didn't have her apron on and for another she was wearing trousers. I thought that was funny because I'd heard my real dad say he'd never allow a woman to wear the trousers again. I thought Blossom must have got to page ten of her book already.

It wasn't Sammy's fault that the tyre burst on his wheelchair just as he was saying,'OK, Snow White, you leg it off into the woods and I'll tell your Evil Step-Dad I've done the business.'

Unfortunately, Sammy almost *did* chop Amy's head off, as when the tyre burst he shot out of control towards her with his axe at the ready. Luckily, Jason blundered on to the stage as he thought Sammy had said 'Guinness' not business. He took the full force of Sammy's little axe in the tankard.

I couldn't wait for my scene. I knew all the cast would be assembled at that moment. Snow White and the Prince were supposed to be signing their partnership contract in her Kindly Mother's castle and everyone was supposed to be celebrating. The Six Small Persons were drinking half-measures, Ms Keegan was doing press-ups stage right, Wanda Walkman had pinched the Prince's little royal handbag to dance around and Mrs Wally had somehow got hold of Mary Hadda's vanity mirror and was polishing it like mad.

Gazza (the Prince) hadn't actually noticed he was supposed to be signing the contract. He was too busy kicking one of the Small Persons' hats around the stage. He looked utterly stunning in his costume. I could hardly take my eyes off him. The Evil Step-Dad (Sharon) had already said her famous lines:

Mirror, Mirror, who's the world's wonder?
Now that Snow White's six foot under?'

And the mirror had replied:

'Evil Step-Dad, you're off your trolley,
Snow White's signing up a wally.'

With that the evil Sharon had to storm in stage left and try to knock Snow White's head off. Snow White would be ducking her head to take a bite of her Snickers bar so Sharon would miss and just at that moment I would try to push past Amy to arrest her. At the back of the hall I could see Jed talking urgently into his mobile phone. I guessed he was ringing Steven Spielberg or someone for advice. Al had met Steven Spielberg in Hollywood — a close encounter, she'd said, when she told us how she'd almost knocked him into the swimming pool with one of her shoulder-pads.

I waited breathlessly in the wings. My great moment! How would Gazza be able to resist me when I got my standing ovation? I could just imagine his sweet, honeyed lips pressed upon mine and his stunned whisper of admiration in my ear.

Outside, I could hear the loud roar of a motor bike engine and guessed a Hell's Angel must have flown in. There was another noise too, coming from behind the scenery. I thought at first it was some more of Al's liberated pigs but all I could smell was the greasepaint that was running off my spot, so it couldn't have been.

I *could* hear Sonia clicking behind me, Mick-the-Dick frantically rehearsing his two words. (Surely he could remember 'Congratulations, Prince' by now, especially as Sonia had written them on a piece of torn paper and pinned it to his false beard.) Jed must be backstage by now because I could hear the whirr of his creative video camera as he recorded the events. What he was doing *behind* the scenery I couldn't quite make out, but who was I, a mere fluffy-slippered Policeperson, to argue?

As I peeped round the curtain, waiting for my cue, I

realized that Al had gone from her Organizer/Boss/ Person-in-Charge/Author/Director/Producer's chair at the front of the house.

I could see my real dad sitting in front of Blossom. I think the top hat belonging to the Artful Dodger costume he wore as a disguise was blocking her view. Then I saw a little careworn hand come up from behind him and knock it off. Blossom waved the hat at me. Just as I waved back, one of my slippers fell off. I kicked the other one off as well. Wearing two would look pretty stupid but wearing only one would look totally weird. It shot across the stage, over the footlights and into the audience. Timmie clambered across several old people and thumped it with the butt of his World War Two reproduction German army rifle. He must have thought it was the cat.

I thought it was a crowd of animal lovers that surged down the aisle but it was only an attempted DIPPO uprising. The rain of chairs and school canteen sandwiches that just missed the heads of the VIPs must have been hurled by the Body Bs and the battered wives. They were pretty good shots. I saw the Mayor step over the bodies on his way to the loo. At least, I think he was off to the loo, although he could have needed some tissue to wipe his secretary's blood from his chain. I could have sworn that sandwich had missed her.

I heard Sonia Scissorhands whisper, 'Out, out, damned spot,' and take off her shoes.

'Phew, Charlie,' she said, making dramatic gestures at the spotlights with her fingernails. 'It ain't half hot, Mum.'

'Sonia,' I whispered. 'Er . . . Miss Scissorhands . . . er . . . I mean, Miss Taylor —'

'Yes,' she interrupted. 'A fine, fine actress. *National Velvet . . . Cleopatra . . . Cat on a Hot Tin Roof* and all those husbands . . . yes indeed, her talents lie in many directions . . . ah, there but for the grace of Form Three go I . . .'

'Sonia,' I repeated, 'could I possibly borrow your shoes?'

'Shoes?' Sonia took a nail file from the golf-bagful she always carried with her in case she broke one. I could only just hear the actors' words above the rasping sound.

Afraid I'd miss my cue, I said hurriedly, 'Yes . . . I couldn't borrow them, could I? I'll look a bit weedy with no shoes on.'

After all, Al had said — 'If you want it, Charlie, go for it.'

'Er . . . if you desire, my dear,' Sonia announced. 'After all, all the world's a stage, and all the men and women merely players,' she smiled at me over her fingernails. '*As You Like It*, you know, darling.'

'Yes,' I said. 'I do like it . . . them . . . In fact I totally adore them. Can I really borrow them?'

I knew that if she said yes, my life would be complete. Who needs the Seven Tips for a Sexy Snog? All I needed was a zitless nose, a pair of heavenly spotted shoes, and the starring role in my mum's panto. (And of course, Gazza's sweet kiss which was inevitable once he realized my charms were greater than those of Manchester United or Sharon Smith dressed as Dame Edna. Mind you, the costume she was wearing to go and try to poison Snow W. was totally ridiculous. Whoever saw Dame Edna in a silver Lycra mini skirt, bikini top, thigh length black leather boots and a collar with studs on? Let alone a whip in one hand and a copy of *Bound for Sexcess* in the other.)

I drew a deep breath and . . . sneezed. Mary Hadda had obviously been powdering her nose. I'd wondered what that cloud of pink dust had been. It was a good job Al was nowhere to be seen. She'd probably have thought Chernobyl had gone up again.

Sonia handed me a ripped tissue. I wiped my nose. Then she dangled her shoes at me. 'Help yourself, Charlie,' she said. 'After all, frailty, thy name is woman.'

97

I hoped Al hadn't heard her sexist remark, but as she was *still* nowhere to be seen, I guessed she hadn't.

I stepped on stage. Everyone turned towards me. Gazza's crown almost fell off when he saw me. He actually stopped kicking the Small Person's hat in and out of Jed's turrets. I knew the shoes looked great, especially with my black stockings (Well . . . one was black. The other one had been eaten by Fiona's hyena who mistook it for a dead snake, so I'd borrowed one of Al's orange ones for the other leg. After all, we all need a bit of colour in our lives.) and tiny Policeperson's mini-skirt. I had polished my constabulary buttons until they reflected my glory.

I thought at first Gazza might sweep me off my spotty shoes and kiss me there and then but he didn't. Still, he would have had to clamber over Amy who had fallen over and couldn't get up and that would have been far too undignified for a prince. So, resigned to having to wait a few minutes longer to feel the sweet caress of his angel lips, I drew a deep breath and said my lines.

'I arrest you, Evil Step-Dad, in the name of the law. After all, women did not suffer for equality just so you blokes could get away with murder.'

Gazza clambered over Amy and strolled royally towards me. I could see wonderment in his glasses. His manly chest heaved with passion and beads of fragrant sweat broke out on his fair, princely brow. I held my arms out . . . Now was the moment . . . I shut my eyes in sweet anticipation (it says in my *Pash Mag.* you're supposed to do that). When I opened them, Gazza was nowhere to be seen. I turned. There he was, the perfect gentleman as ever, helping the Evil Step-Dad hold up her bikini top. Unfortunately, Sonia had been giving stage directions in the wings and had accidentally cut one of the straps.

There was a moment's silence. The success of the

whole performance was held in the balance. Off-stage I could hear a panting noise and wondered if Mr Donovan was dying of thirst. I decided to improvise, to use my experience as a Star to turn the evening into a block-busting success.

I put my hands on Sharon's shoulder.

'Will you kindly accompany me to the station?' I said assertively. 'Or else I'll have to call for reinforcements.'

'It's not you what needs reinforcements,' Sharon giggled as Gazza lost his grip and her Dame Edna bikini top fell off completely. 'It's me.'

With that the house erupted. I turned to see a bunch of old folk haring down the aisle towards the stage. I thought at first it was my standing (well, running) ovation. But then I saw they were waving their Euro-Dis flags and badges at me. One was wearing a Cruella de Vil costume but the wig had fallen to one side showing his bald head. Another looked really neat in 3-D glasses and Peter Pan hat, although when he tried to fly up on the stage he fell and crushed one of Deathshead Condom's sporrans.

'It's her!' one sweet old person yelled, waving a Mary Poppins umbrella. 'It's her what . . .'

I didn't wait to hear what I'd done. I mean, if you were on stage in fantastically spotted high-heeled shoes and a policeperson's uniform pinched from the High Security Remand Centre and a horde of pensioners bent on revenge for Paddy Powell's inadvertent trespass into their territory were surging towards you, what would you do?

Scarper, of course.

But I didn't get far. For one thing I tripped over Paddy Powell. I knew ten o'clock was past his bedtime but hadn't realized he'd actually fallen asleep off-stage. I think the crunching noise was the sound of his charming Snow White's mother's crystal lager glass disintegrating beneath my spotty shoes. Then I got caught up with Ms Keegan doing her warm-down on her mountain bike. Just outside the door I could see a couple of St John Ambulancepersons loading someone on to a stretcher. I heard Al's voice.

'Now be careful with him,' she shouted from a make-shift bed in the caretaker's cupboard. 'He's had a very nasty shock.'

To my surprise, Nurse F. was there, helping Al sit up. She quickly ran to take the video camera from Jed's shaking hand before they carted him off.

'I hope he didn't miss anything,' my mum said. Then she saw me standing there resplendent in Sonia's spotties.

'Charlie!' She grinned delightedly as Nurse F. took off her apron and went to wash her hands.

Al handed me a bundle. I thought at first it was a present to honour my success.

The bundle moved and a squeak came from inside.

'Here you are, Charlie,' Al grinned again. 'The surprise Small Person. A bit early, but we must be unpredictable if we are to succeed.'

I looked down. My eyes must have been wide with wonder.

Yes . . . you've guessed it.

There, the studs on its tiny leather jacket reflecting the spotlight of stardom was . . .

THE BABY!

10

The baby was called Harley Elvis. Al said it was because the first thing she saw after the baby's birth was the midwife's Harley Davidson parked under the stairs. Gazza said later it was a good job the baby wasn't born in the shack after all. Otherwise it might have been called Chicken Pooh.

Mum took a swig of champagne and handed the bottle back to Mr Donovan. 'Well,' she said, nodding her head at me. 'Take Harley on stage, Charlie. It's time for her to make her first appearance.'

Everyone on stage was looking a bit confused. Half the cast had disappeared when Snow White had stripped off her tent to throw over the Evil Step-Dad. We found Sharon still under it later, crying because her bikini top was covered in toffee and was stuck to the stage. Ms Keegan tried to prise it off with her mountain bike pump but only ended up getting air up her leotard.

The horde of folk from the Day Centre seemed a bit confused too. They stood dejectedly in front of the stage. One or two had switched off their hearing aids when the band started to play another number. They soon stopped when one old person hooked the plug off the speakers with her flick knife.

Then, someone in the audience, I think it was Blossom, started clapping and stamping their feet. I saw the Artful Dodger artfully dodge away clutching his copy of the *Satellite Times*. If he thought there was a TV in the staff room he'd be really choked. It had been pinched ages ago, together with the one-arm bandit and the cigarette machine. Paddy had denied all knowledge although I did see him trying to buy a crate of lager in the Off Licence with four hundred silver tokens.

Anyway, my real dad didn't get far. I saw Blossom throw a lasso. It slipped neatly over his neck. She pulled it tight and roped him in. There must have been a chapter on cowboys in my mum's book. My real dad looked really funny with a blue face, although it soon turned red again when Timmie threw up all over his gun. I guessed he must have eaten one of the canteen sandwiches the CRAPPS had used as missiles.

Then the cry went up. 'Producer! Producer!' and Al came on stage. One of the DIPPOS ran off to the Headmaster's office to get her a chair. I trotted behind her on my (well, Sonia's) gorgeously spotted shoes, cradling my sweet darling little sister in my arms. Someone had cleaned her face with recycled tissue.

Gazza was beside me.

'Isn't she gorgeous, Gaz?' I whispered. 'Just like we'll have one day.'

Gaz wrinkled up his heavenly nose. 'What's that pong? She filled her nappy?'

'No, Gaz,' I giggled, realizing for the first time that my fab shoes made me almost as tall as he was. I could see my reflection in his rose-tinted lenses. I gulped and looked closer. My spot had gone. It must have shot off when Mary's powder made me sneeze. I smiled into Gazza's angel eyes. 'It's my perfume,' I said sweetly. 'Don't you like it? I found it in the pocket of my Police-person's outfit.' I took the spray out and showed him.

'That's not perfume,' Gazza said, 'it's anti-mugging

102

spray. My mum carries it when she goes to church.'

'Oh,' I shrugged. 'Well, at least it works. No one's mugged me, have they? I hope it's ozone friendly.'

I realized that Al was giving a speech. I just hoped the Headmaster's chair didn't collapse before she finished.

'I'm afraid the real hero of the hour has been carted off to casualty . . .' she was saying.

I heard Mick-the-Dick whisper behind me. 'That's my mum's favourite programme.'

Paddy took hold of his Small Person's tunic. 'Yeah?' he said in his Gentle Snow White's Mother's voice. 'So?'

Sammy poked Paddy in the kneecap with his axe. 'Leave him alone, Paddy, or I'll chop your tattoo off.'

Paddy looked scared and sat down on his crate.

'But I know you'll all wish him a speedy recovery,' Al was saying. 'Giving birth is a very traumatic time for a father, you know. It's a good job we women are there to keep the ship afloat.'

'What's she saying?' Wanda shouted.

'Nothing important,' I said. 'Something about joining the Navy, I think. It must be because Jed lent her his diving gear when our shack got flooded out.'

'Pardon?' Wanda said.

'Hear, hear,' a voice came from the audience. I knew it was Blossom that time because I saw her trying to prise an old person's ear trumpet off Timmie's head. It came off with a pop and I saw Blossom swipe Timmie with my real dad's copy of *Playgirl International*.

'Do you want to hold her?' I whispered to Gazza. Before he could back away I popped the baby gently into his arms. He pushed aside her little red-spotted scarf and peered into her sweet face.

'She looks like your mum,' he said, gazing in awe as she dribbled on to his hand.

'Rubbish,' I insisted. 'She's beautiful.'

*   *   *

103

I realized that Al was thanking everyone for making the production such a success.

'Of course,' she was going, 'one or two of the men helped too.' She slapped Jason on the back. When he picked himself up he reeled off stage left. I heard later he'd made it all the way to the Duck and Shotgun before passing out. 'To say nothing of my female friends who routed the DIPPOS.'

A cheer went up.

Just then there was a shout from the back of the hall and a couple of DIPPOS charged down one of the aisles brandishing helmets and riot shields.

'Quick!' Al yelled. 'All CRAPPS on deck.'

I thought the missile that came sailing towards us was a bomb. Gazza was still holding my precious sister so he couldn't have thrown himself in front of me to save me being injured. I skipped neatly in front of him and headed the missile off with my helmet. I heard Gazza gasp with admiration as it sailed back into the DIPPOS and exploded with an almighty bang.

'Goal!' Gazza yelled, jumping up and down with excitement. He handed Harley back to me while he crawled around looking for his crown. I found it later tucked inside Harley's little black shawl. Her little rosebud mouth was all gold where she'd been sucking it.

When the air cleared I realized the missile had only been a Monsieur Mickey Mouse balloon filled with water. The last I saw of the DIPPOS was them being marched off by the Body Bs looking rather wet. One of them was being beaten around the head by the old lady bereft of her Mickey balloon. I heard her swear at the DIPPO as he offered her a twenty quid note.

'Then,' Al went on as if nothing had happened, 'there's my other daughter, Charlie. She had her part to play. After all, where would we be without the law, huh?'

'She sure did,' an old person yelled from the front.

'Oh, no. . .' I tried to hide behind Gazza but it was no good, they'd spotted me.

Then the pensioners' spokesperson leapt on to the stage, a huge bunch of flowers in her arms.

Mum smiled and held out her arms. 'There's really no need . . .' she began. 'Women have babies every day. It's no big deal.' She turned. 'Although Harley did weigh about ten pounds, I reckon.' The spokesperson dodged past her and came towards me.

'These,' she said, fluttering her false eyelashes, and waving her be-jewelled fingers, 'are for this young lady . . .'

'Young lady . . .' my mum said. 'But . . . that's Charlie!'

'For Charlie . . .' the old folk's spokesperson curtsied in front of me as if I was Lady Di or someone. 'For being so brave.'

'Brave . . . ?' I glanced at Gazza. He was looking at me. I think it was admiration in his eyes, although it could have been smudged eyeshadow. Mary had certainly done a wonderful job with his make-up.

'Yes,' the spokesperson went on, 'for pretending to be a real copper and frightening off that escaped hi-jacker.'

'Hi-jacker . . . ?'

The SP smiled at me. Her gold teeth glinted in the spotlight like the treasure of Aladdin's cave. 'Yeah, he'd escaped from the Remand Centre and almost pinched our mini-bus *and* the proceeds of the Sponsored Strip we'd held to raise funds for our next visit to Euro-Dis.'

'Oh,' I said. Then I remembered the bloke outside the Old Folk's Day Centre who'd shoved a bag and keys into my arms. He must have been who she meant. You could have knocked me down with one of the feathers in Paddy's head-dress.

The SP thrust the flowers into my arms. She turned to the audience. 'This young lady deserves a standing ovation. Without her we may not have got another go on Buffalo Bill's Wagon Ride of Death.'

'Not 'arf she don't,' Gaz said. 'Did you see that

header? What a goal!' He began chanting angelically, 'CHAR-LIE, CHAR-LIE . . . CHAR-LIE.'

I heard Al behind me. 'Of course,' she was saying, 'I always knew she had talent. I said she should be an actor. To hell with structural engineering.' She sighed. 'I wish Jed was here, it's almost time to feed the baby.'

I tried to tell them I just happened to be on the spot, that I wasn't pretending to be anything, but they wouldn't listen.

When the applause died down and people began wandering off, I took off Sonia's shoes.

'Here you are, Miss,' I said sadly. 'Thanks for letting me borrow them.'

Sonia waved her hands dangerously. 'Keep them, Charlie.' She balanced them delicately on her fingernails. 'Fame will not be easy . . . I should know . . . But always remember the web of our life is of a mingled yarn, good and ill together . . . *All's Well That Ends Well* . . . you know,' she whispered, 'William Shakespeare.'

'Never 'eard of 'im,' Paddy yawned and fell off his crate.

Al had decided to hold the after-panto party at the shack. We'd stopped off at casualty to pick up Jed. There was a queue of DIPPOS outside the hospital so we guessed most of them had got pneumonia or mud-poisoning.

'Serves them right,' Al remarked. 'Anyone who doesn't wear waterproofs in this climate's asking for trouble.'

Jed came out clutching his Laura Ashley for Men cosmetic bag. Al hugged him. When he recovered his breath he said, 'Is it a boy?'

Mum smiled. 'Now don't panic, sweetie. It's a girl. Her name's Harley Elvis.'

'Look what I've got, Jed,' I said, holding up my wonderful shoes.

'Oh, Charlie,' he sighed laboriously. 'I didn't know Oxfam opened this late at night.'

I wore them with my pink flouncy frock.

I managed to scrub off the smell of the anti-mugging spray with one of Harley's fragrant bottom wipes and Al lent me some of her Body Shop MaMa Toto all-over mother's body rub. It smelt great. I couldn't quite reach all-over but didn't think it mattered. Jed said you're supposed to rub it on the baby but I didn't think Harley would mind. She was so overwhelmed by her black-draped orange box she cried for an hour.

I tried to tell my mum about the hi-jacker and how I was only picking up some McDonald's throw-aways outside the Day Centre but she wouldn't listen.

'You're too modest, Charlie,' she said. 'We women must tell the world of our achievements. After all, look at the Queen, at Cleopatra, at Lady Godiva. If you've got it, Charlie, show it.'

'Show what?' I said, thinking of my hardly-grown chest. I mean, Cleopatra showed hers, so did Lady Godiva, but I've never seen the Queen go topless.

'Your bravery, Charlie. You haven't got much else.'

As usual, my mum hadn't listened to a word I'd said.

Just then everyone started arriving. Jed had dressed Harley in her best clothes. Her little suffragette costume looked lovely with the yellow and black striped bonnet I'd knitted. Even the AA Recovery Man who had to pull everyone's cars out of the mud said she looked great.

It was a bit of a squash in the front room. Amy was trying to dance with Mick-the-Dick but her picnic basket kept getting in the way. Mrs Wally came in in her best cocktail dress. I thought at first her trolley was loaded full of cleaning stuff but she'd picked up Mr Donovan on her way past the pub. I think he must have thought her bottle of bleach was gin but luckily Blossom knocked it out of his hand before he could take a swig. His Father Christmas outfit looked really strange with white blobs all down the front.

'Where's my real dad?' I asked. 'Not baby-sitting is he?'

Blossom smiled. 'You must be joking, Charlie, I've only got to chapter ninety-six. He's hiding in the outside loo.'

'Oh,' I said, 'he'll be safe there. Jed's bought Mum a porta-potti as a Congratulations on the Birth of your Daughter present.'

Blossom went off to watch Sonia Scissorhands' manicure demonstration. I warned her not to sit too close. She'd got one of my real dad's fair-isle tank tops on and he'd be furious if it got torn.

When the old folk arrived things really livened up. It was a job to make yourself heard over their Singa-longa-Guns'n'Roses tape. Deathshead Condom were quite put out and retired to the village church to read their black magic comics.

'Let's go upstairs,' Gazza whispered, 'I've got something to ask you.'

My heart missed a beat. The Seven Tips for a Sexy Snog flashed through my mind. We'd had a couple of vegetarian sausages so that was OK. There was music, fairly soft lights (the midwife had insisted we got jumbo sized candles), I'd rubbed my body with perfume. I'd shared a caffeine-free diet-Coke with Amy. Well . . . I'd sucked what was left out of her straw. I couldn't actually remember what the other one was. All I needed now was the whispered promise . . .

We clambered up the ladder. Through the hole in the wall (which was going to be a window when Al got round to putting the frame in) I could see Wanda doing the twist in the vegetable patch with four policemen trying to hear the music. I felt sure the Body Bs shouldn't really have been chopping down trees to use as dumb-bells. I didn't really think that was the way to preserve our rural heritage. Somehow, that night I just didn't care. Anyway, Sammy shouldn't have been waving his axe and egging them on like that.

I thought it was the Headmaster arriving on Ms Keegan's crossbar but I wasn't sure. Even Paddy seemed to be enjoying himself kicking hell out of the farmer's haystack, and I was sure it was Mary Hadda and her sports car boyfriend parked in the darkest corner of the field.

There was a delicious smell from the kitchen and I thought Rosa was cooking one of her yummy West Indian meals. I certainly hadn't seen any of our free-range hens, free ranging round the front room for a while.

I led Gazza into my room. Downstairs I could hear grunts as Mum gave a re-run of Harley's birth, or it could have been the pigs trying to get into the shack. I think they'd got a bit fed up with freedom since the women from Mum's tap dancing class used their backs to practise on.

'Well . . .?' I looked at Gazza sexily. My green ribbon fell over one mascaraed eye and I brushed it back impatiently. I didn't want anything to cloud my vision of romance. 'What was it you wanted to ask me?'

'I want . . .' he hesitated. I think his glasses misted up because he was getting excited. (We'd learned in Personal Development that feeling sexy makes blokes perspire.) Although it could have been ice as it was about ten degrees below freezing in my room.

He only moved away a little bit when I put my arms round him. I guessed that was because the bones of my pre-formed bra were sticking into his manly chest.

'I want you . . .' he stammered. He pushed his crumpled crown to the back of his angel head and fiddled passionately with his little fake fur Prince's jacket.

109

At last . . . he wanted me! He really wanted me! All my dreams were coming true. I had a baby. I was a star. I had my heavenly shoes and now that first kiss . . . I knew it was going to be the most romantic, beautiful night of my life. I stretched out my multi-coloured legs to admire my spotty footwear. I imagined Gazza's sensuous lips getting closer . . . closer . . . his rugged, granite-jawed features bright with adoration . . . I drifted away on a golden chariot of passion (I'd read that bit in a Mills and Boon book). I heard angels chanting (or it could have been Rosa's kids doing their synchronized rap . . . *or* my real dad's portable telly in the outside loo) . . . the ringing of bells, the drums of love were sounding in my ears. I knew I would soon be reaching that moment of fulfilment my mum was always on about . . .

'I want you to . . . join the football team,' Gazza blurted. 'That header you did on stage was really magic.'

Before I had time to surrender to his wishes I heard a voice.

'Charlie!' My mum's booted feet drummed up the ladder. 'Didn't you hear the phone? That was Fiona. Apparently the DIPPOS have rallied and are regrouping their forces. They're resorting to underhand tactics. One of them has kidnapped her hyena and is holding him to ransom.'

'Handsome . . . ?' I said, trying to hear her properly over the music. 'Yes, Gazza's the most gorgeous . . . handsome . . .'

'No, Charlie. Ransom.' Her new-mother's bosom heaved with anger. 'Until we agree to stage *Cinderella* next year with evil ugly *sisters!*'

'Well,' I said, 'what's wrong with that?'

Mum tutted. I think she would have fallen off the ladder if there hadn't been six or seven Body Bs supporting her. 'Honestly, Charlie, you might be a heroine but you really are a bit thick.'

'Thanks,' I said sweetly. I knew new mothers (and New Men) could be a bit temperamental.

'Don't you see, Charlie. We must protect Harley from the evils of sexism. We must ensure that vile step-fathers continue to be exposed.'

I heard Sharon Smith giggle from under the ladder. When I looked she was trying on Jed's designer gardener's dungarees. I wouldn't have thought it was necessary for Jed himself to be actually adjusting the straps, but still . . .

'Yes,' Mum was going. 'Our action group will be called Females Against Bigotry.'

'Fab,' Gazza whispered sexily.

I could feel his sweet angel breath on my neck. Or maybe it was the draught from the hole in the roof?

'. . . totally fab.'

END